MW01205717

POOR as CHURCH MICE

POOR as OOR CHURCH MICE

ROSELYN OGDEN MILLER

Dageforde Publishing, Inc

Copyright 2000 by Roselyn Ogden Miller. All rights reserved. No part of this publication may be reproduced, stored in a retrieval system, or transmitted in any form or by any means, electronic, mechanical, photocopied, recorded, or otherwise, without the prior written permission of the publisher.

ISBN 1-886225-57-5

Cover design and illustrations by Janet Nelson Miller, daughter-in-law of the author. Janet says she was born with drawing pencils in her hand.

Cover production by Angie Johnson Art Productions

Library of Congress Cataloging-in-Publication Data

Miller, Roselyn Ogden, 1936-
   Poor as church mice / Roselyn Ogden Miller.
     p. cm.
   Summary: Twelve-year-old Nora and her younger sister and brothers struggle to stay together and to someday be reunited with their mother after they travel from New York City to Nebraska on the orphan train in 1870.
   ISBN 1-886225-57-5 (alk. paper)
   [1. Orphan trains—Fiction. 2. Brothers and sisters—Fiction. 3. Poverty—Fiction.]   I. Title.
   PZ7.M633375 Po 2000
   [Fic]—dc21.

                                   00-03-4070

Dageforde Publishing, Inc.
122 South 29th Street
Lincoln, Nebraska 68510
Phone: (402) 475-1123 Fax: (402) 475-1176
email: info@dageforde.com

**Visit our web site at
www.dageforde.com**

Printer in the United States of America
10 9 8 7 6 5 4 3 2 1

This book is dedicated to my granddaughters TJ, Kalee, Trista, and Courtney who gave me hope by listening as I read it to them in its earliest stages.

CHAPTER 1

Nora sat in the high-backed wooden rocker in the cold front room of the home she shared with her ill mother, younger sister and brothers. Her heavy auburn braid hung like a long question mark down the front of the faded, frayed quilt she had wrapped around her thin, skimpy nightgown. She waited for her brother Nils to return from a day of finding jobs to help pay the rent for next month. She hoped he had done well selling newspapers at the corner of York and Ohio Streets. With what he could earn and what Mrs. Florenz paid her for house cleaning, it should be enough.

She pulled at her braid. If only she could find work closer to home. She wished she could find more houses to clean. She hated the long walk that showed her the hundreds of homeless children that lived in the streets. Many because of fathers dying in the War between the States and the industrial revolution where steam engines replaced the hand work of men and women and many times, children.

Nora knew if they couldn't earn enough money to pay the rent, they too, would be living in the streets. But New York City had grown so much in the past few years, and now in 1870, there must be many homes to clean, loads of coal for Nils to unload, or newspapers to sell.

Snuggling down into the quilt Nora tried to remember the happy times in their home when there was a blazing fire in the fireplace. Each child was wrapped in an eiderdown filled quilt Grandma had made. Warm and happy they listened to the stories Mama told of when she and Papa were young. Nora regretted selling the quilts but the money had paid for the first month's rent. What would she use for next month's rent if Nils didn't find work?

She shook her head. She wasn't going to worry about it. Instead she was going to think about the family before Papa left for the War between the States to be a doctor to the wounded soldiers...before Mama got sick and stayed in bed all day...before Grandma Tucker died. Five years was a long time to be responsible for helping care for the children and Mama.

Slowly her eyes closed and she slept. The weariness of caring for her family faded. She once again looked like a twelve-, almost thirteen-year-old girl.

POOR AS CHURCH MICE

A loud bang on the front door woke her with a start, and she bumped her head on the rocker. She sat quietly for a minute, trying to identify the noise. More banging! Like a shot she raced across the cold linoleum floor on her bare feet. The quilt tangled around her legs; she untangled it and threw it around her shoulders. The cold floor encouraged her to move even faster.

"Darn it," she muttered as she pulled the door open. "Stop poun..." She saw a large, beefy fist raised to strike the door again and ducked.

"Sorry, Miss. I wasn't sure anyone heard me knock, being so late at night and all," said a gruff voice.

Nora looked into a rough craggy face, then let her blue eyes scan the blue uniform of a New York City policeman. She saw her brother held fast by the collar of his threadbare coat. She cringed when she saw how the sleeves came above his wrists and the shoulders pulled tight even though he was standing still.

"Does he live here?"

Nora's attention was brought back to the policeman. "Yes, yes, he does," she replied.

Nils squirmed and tried to free himself from the policeman's grip. "Let me go," he cried.

"Nils, what have you done?" asked Nora, stepping onto the porch. When she turned to pull the door shut, she discovered Amanda and Charley in the doorway.

"What's wrong, Nora?" asked nine-year-old Charley, hopping from one foot to the other.

3

"Who woke me up?" whined Amanda, rubbing her eyes.

"Never mind. You two go back to bed. We'll be along in a minute. Go on now. You'll catch your death of cold," commanded Nora, pulling the door shut. "Now see what you've done. You woke the family!"

"Sorry, Miss, I'm just doing my duty. Are your mother and father home?"

Nora's teeth chattered from the cold and fear. "My...our mother is in bed. She had a long hard day at work, and my father...er, works the night shift at the railroad yards. What did Nils do?"

"I caught him stealing coal chunks off the pile at Mr. Claussen's store. You tell your folks if I catch him again I'll not be bringing him home. It will be the children's work farm for him," said the policeman giving Nils a shove.

"Good night, sir," she called after the policeman's retreating back.

Nora followed Nils into the house and, with her fingers to her lips, tiptoed to the doorway of her mother's bedroom and listened.

"Who was at the door, Nora? Is something wrong?" a weak voice called.

Nora went to her mother. She fluffed up the pillow and smoothed the counterpane. "No, Mother," she said. "Nils thought the door was locked, but it was just stuck."

"What time is it, dear?"

"About eight o'clock," replied Nora.

"Oh. Be sure you children get to bed soon. With school tomorrow, you need your sleep."

"Yes, Mother. Good night," said Nora, closing the door softly.

"Nora," said Charley, "are we really going to school tomorrow?"

"Are you going to school and leaving me alone?" cried five-year-old Amanda, clinging to Nora.

Nora glared at them, put her finger to her lips and pointed to the hallway that led to the kitchen and the back bedroom where the boys slept. She took Amanda by the hand, led her into their bedroom and tucked her into bed.

"Nora, why did the policeman come home with Nils? Was he lost?" asked Amanda snuggling down under the worn, faded quilt.

"Yes, he was lost," replied Nora. "Now go to sleep. I'll be back as soon as I put Charley back to bed."

Nora crept across the cold linoleum floor of the living room to listen at her mother's door. All was quiet so she ran quickly to the boys' room. They had crawled into the double bed. Nils' face was to the wall.

"Nils didn't put his nightshirt on, Nora," declared Charley.

"Shut up, tattle-tale!" shouted Nils. "Nora's not my boss, and Mama is too sick to care. What about those lies you told the policeman and Mama tonight?" He glared at Nora. "'Mama tired after a hard day's work, and Papa at a night job!' It's been years since Mama even took care of us, and Papa died four years ago when Amanda was a baby. As for going to school to-morrow, we haven't been able to go since Grandma Tucker died two years ago, and you took over the job of caring for us."

Nora climbed on the foot of the boys' bed, tucked her feet under their quilts and rewrapped her quilt around her shoulders. Tears slowly slid down her cheeks. She looked at Nils. "What was I supposed to do Nils? Tell him Mama never gets out of bed, and we don't have a Papa because he was killed in the War? They'd put her in a hospital and send us to the children's work farm. We'd be separated. You know Mama promised Papa we would stay together no matter what happened. We have to keep her promise for her. I had to lie to the policeman and Mama. She is too sick to be worried about us not going to school. It's your fault, too, Nils. Why did a policeman bring you home at eleven o'clock at night?"

Nils slowly lay back down in the bed. His bright red hair against the pillowcase was so like Papa's, thought Nora as she shivered in her skimpy nightgown.

"Well?" she asked.

Nils sat up again. His bright blue eyes looked sad as he said, "You aren't the only one who hears Mama cough. I know she needs to be warm to get well. I was only trying to get some coal to heat the house."

"Oh, Nils, I'm sorry! I should have known. But what happened to the newspapers you were supposed to sell on John's corner?"

"Yeah, well, Scruffy Thornberg had other ideas. He put one of his boys on that corner and...he took my newspapers." Nils slid down and hid his face in the pillow.

Nora saw his shoulders shaking. "Don't worry, Nils, we'll think of something. Just promise me you won't steal again. Good night," she said, tucking the quilt around the boys' shoulders.

"Nora," said Nils. I heard a bunch of guys are going to unload a carload of coal for Mr. Claussen tomorrow. Maybe I can get a job there."

"Yes, maybe. I've been promised work at the banker's house. Mrs. Florenz, who I work for now, said Mrs. Buckingham needs a girl for a week while her hired girl is gone. I will be able to keep working. Then Mrs. Florenz will be back from her visit to her sister's, and I will work there again. Don't worry Nils, we'll manage. Good night."

Nora hurried to her bedroom. She spread the quilt from her shoulders over the sleeping Amanda and crawled in beside her. It must be nearly midnight, she thought wearily, closing her eyes for the hundredth time. She kept thinking of the lies she had told the policeman and her mother. She shook her head and snuggled against Amanda. Amanda cried out. Nora patted her until she felt her relax. Then gave herself up to her thoughts.

She couldn't remember when Mama had spent a full day on her feet. She had spent many hours resting after Amanda's birth, so Papa asked his widowed mother to live with them to help with the children and the housework. Then Papa had gone to fight in the War between the States and had been killed in the second battle of Bull Run. After Mama had read his name on the list of men killed in action, she went to bed and stayed there. Nora helped Grandmother more and more, until she finally took over all the household tasks. Grandmother had died nearly two years ago.

Nora had never worried about money. Papa had sold the house and furniture with the stipulation his family could live there until he came home from the war; then they would buy a new house. But Papa didn't come home, and the money ran out in the special account Papa and the banker had set up.

Last month, the man who had bought the house stopped by to collect rent money from Nora. He told Nora the banker had said there was no more money. Nora went to see Banker Buckingham; he was sorry, but he could no longer help. She went to see the grocer. He said he would accept any of Mama's china, lamps, jewelry or other household items that the landlord didn't own as payment for groceries. There were few pretty items left to sell for rent or groceries. She was afraid of what would happen to them with winter coming. And now the policeman would be sure to watch for Nils.

There would be no money unless the banker's wife hired Nora because Mrs. Florenz had taken that week off to spend with her sister. She planned to stop at the banker's house on the way home from Mrs. Florenz's tomorrow. Mrs. Florenz was sure Nora would get the job. That would pay the rent, and the ruby brooch she had found in Mama's bureau would buy groceries. If Nils didn't get work, he could at least find some wooden crates to chop up at Mr. Claussen's. What more could she do? Who could she ask for help?

Grandma Tucker always said they were poor as church mice, but each child had a crowning glory. When Nora asked what she meant, Grandma replied with a twinkle in her eye. "Well, you know the food in a church is the bread used in the Lord's Supper or Communion, and no one lets a crumb of that fall. So, if you are a mouse living in a church you would be a very poor, skinny mouse."

"Yes," replied Nora, smiling, "you'd be a very poor mouse. But what about the crowning glory?"

"Well," Grandma mused, "when I was a child it meant something special about a person- a special gift that often got them out of trouble. But now I just see something very special about each of you children and that's what I call your crowning glory."

Grandma's was her faith in God, no matter what the problem. Well, that might work for Grandma Tucker, but what about a twelve-year-old? Did she have enough faith? "Please Lord..." she whispered as she closed her eyes.

CHAPTER 2

The next morning, Nora and Amanda kissed their mama good-bye as they left to go to Mrs. Florenz's house to work.

"Have a good day at school, dears," said Mother.

"Charley, come into the kitchen; I want to talk to you," said Nora.

Charley lifted his thin body out of the overstuffed chair and followed the girls.

"Now remember, Charley, if Mama asks why you didn't go to school, tell her you think you are catching a cold," instructed Nora.

He shrugged his thin shoulders and his oversized sweater sleeve unrolled. Charley rolled them up again.

"She won't ask me, she'll just want to know when Papa is coming home and why Grandma Tucker doesn't come when she calls," he said.

Nora patted his shoulder and said sadly, "I know, Charley, but we have to pretend. Otherwise we'll all end up on the children's work farm. Nils hopes to unload coal for Mr. Claussen today. Maybe he'll be able to bring a big chunk home. Mama will want milk toast. Remember, just heat the milk a little so it doesn't taste burned. You can have two slices of toast. Amanda and I will be working at Mrs. Florenz's all day and plan to stop at Mrs. Buckingham's to see about work at her house next week while Mrs. Florenz is in Albany. See you later," said Nora as she opened the door to scoot Amanda out.

Holding Amanda's hand, they began their long walk to Mrs. Florenz's. Once again Nora tried not to look at the dirty ragged children and their meager possessions. They had to stay clear of the police, for when they didn't have a home, they were taken to the poor farm to help care for the poor elderly. She shivered. Last night, when a policeman had brought Nils home she realized how careful they had to be. As long as they could both find work for rent and food....

Nora suddenly became aware of Amanda tugging at her coat.

"Nora, aren't we going to Mrs. Florenz's house?" demanded Amanda.

"What? Oh, yes, of course we are."

"Well, we passed her gate, and you kept right on going."

"Oh, silly me," laughed Nora as she ran back to the gate.

POOR AS CHURCH MICE

Nora scrubbed the kitchen floor on her hands and knees. The shiny linoleum was easy to clean since only Mrs. Florenz and her cat, Puddin, walked on it.

She sat back a minute and watched Amanda cutting out paper dolls from a magazine. Amanda loved to pretend with the make believe people. She had names for each of them. They always had a mama and a papa and were rich with lots of good food to eat.

Nora listened as Amanda began talking to the little girl paper doll she held up. "I'll call you Tabatha, and your mama will be strong and not sick, and she'll brush your hair into long ringlets like mine. But she won't pull your hair and make it hurt like Nora does."

Nora felt the blood rush to her face. She was rough with Amanda's hair, but it just seemed to tangle so easily. There was never enough time in the morning to brush it thoroughly and still have time to do all the housework. If only she could stay at home and not worry about money.

Nora dumped her scrub water out the back door. It was going to be very cold walking home, but at least they could stop and get warm at Mrs. Buckingham's.

Mrs. Florenz came into the kitchen. "Nora, I have some food I'm sending home with you in my in my favorite basket that my son Jim made me before he left for the War between the States. No sense letting it spoil while I'm gone." She handed Nora the basket, tucking a snowy white tea towel around the food. Nora resisted the temptation to peek at what Mrs. Florenz had packed.

"Now remember, you stop at Mrs. Buckingham's and get warm. I told her what a good worker you are, and that Amanda stays with you and is no trouble at all. Then I'll see you again the following Monday. Good-bye now."

Nora wrapped a scarf around Amanda's head and neck, then put her oversized coat on her. Amanda stuffed her paper dolls in her coat pocket.

Nora shrugged into her coat, pulled it tight across her chest, and buttoned it. She saw Mrs. Florenz staring at her shabby, too-tight coat and ducked her head.

"Good-bye, Mrs. Florenz. Thank you for the basket of food and Amanda's paper dolls. We'll be back next Monday."

Nora opened the door and a blast of wind took her breath away. Pushing Amanda ahead of her, she began the long trip home. Thank goodness they were stopping at Mrs. Buckingham's! With her basket on her arm and her hands stuffed in her coat pockets, she walked as fast as she could without leaving Amanda behind. With a sigh of relief, she pushed the black wrought iron gate open and hurried Amanda to Mrs. Buckingham's door.

"Nora, let's go home. I'm cold," whined Amanda while they waited for someone to answer the knock.

"I know, Sweetie," Nora answered as she snuggled Amanda against her.

The door opened and Nora looked up into the stern face of a woman. Her black hair was drawn back so tight it made her eyes look slanted. "Yes, can I help you?" she asked.

"Mrs. Florenz said you were looking for kitchen help this week while your regular girl is gone. I'd like to apply for the job," replied Nora.

Nora watched the woman's eyes shift to her shabby coat and bare, rough red hands, then to Amanda. "What do you do with her while you work?" she demanded.

"This is Amanda, my little sister. I don't have anyone to leave her with. She is really very well-behaved and plays quietly while I work," explained Nora.

"Well, you stop by tomorrow, and we will discuss it." She began to shut the door.

"But, ma'am, can't I talk to the lady of the house? Mrs. Florenz assured me..."

"Miss, I said I would take care of the matter. Now, if you want the job, you will stop by tomorrow morning at seven, and I will tell you if you are hired. Good day." The door shut quietly, but firmly in Nora's face.

Amanda began to cry. "I thought we were going to get warm there."

"Never mind, Sweetie, we'll go home and see how Charley and Mama are doing. Maybe Nils got a large piece of coal to put in Mama's stove, and we can get warm while we talk to her," promised Nora, taking

15

Amanda's mittened hand and running down the street to get warm.

"Hello, everyone, we're home!" called Nora as she closed the door.

A policeman stepped out of Mama's bedroom door.

"Oh, no," cried Nora. "Nils, where's Nils?"

"Here I am, Nora," called Nils from the back bedroom. "Charley and I are getting our things together. The policeman is taking Mama to the hospital, and we all have to go to the Children's Home."

She saw her mother being carried out on a stretcher by two white-coated men.

"Mama!" Nora ran to her. The men waited as Nora kissed her mother.

"Don't worry, Mama. I'll work hard so we can bring you home and stay together as a family like you promised Papa," she cried, holding her mother's hand.

A large hand on her shoulder startled her, and she let go of her mother's hand. The policeman who had brought Nils home last night smiled sadly at her and nodded to the men. She raised her hands to strike the policeman, but he held them down and pulled her against his chest. She relaxed and cried, her tears wetting the blue wool of his uniform.

"There, there, Miss, 'tis the best solution. Now she can get well and you tykes can be warm and well fed at the Children's Home."

"But, won't Nils have to go to the work farm?" she asked, lifting her tear-stained face. "You said if you caught him stealing again he would have to go there."

"Oh, but I didn't catch him stealing, Miss."

"Then why...?"

" 'Twas Mr. Claussen, the grocer. He said he hadn't seen you in for groceries and was concerned about you," explained the policeman.

"Oh," said Nora. "But can't we stay? Now that Mama is taken care of, Charley can find work, too. I know we can earn enough now. I have a promise of a job tomorrow."

"Sorry, Miss, but the law says children must be cared for by adults," explained the policeman.

"Only if they get caught," muttered Nora, thinking of the many street children who had been abandoned by their parents or were orphaned by the war.

Nora went to the rocking chair where Amanda was curled up in a ball, her blue eyes big. "Come, Mandy," she said.

"Where did those men take Mama?" she asked.

"To get well," replied Nora, brushing the red-brown hair out of Amanda's eyes.

Her shoulders sagged, and the long braid that hung down her back felt twice as heavy. She pulled it over her shoulder, smiling a secret smile. She thought to herself, "Don't worry, Mama, I'll always remember what you promised Papa before he left for the war, that we would stay together as a family no matter what. And like Grandma said, we all have our crowning glories to be proud of. If we just remember that, and that we were special to Grandma, Papa and are to you, Mama, we can do anything we have to. Grandma and you had your faith in God. Do you still believe in Him, Mama? I find it hard to believe. First you got sick, then Papa died, and Grandma died, and now we have to leave our home and be separated from you. I know you said my hair was my crowning glory because Papa loved how beautiful it was, just like yours, a rich dark auburn and so heavy."

"Miss, if you will pack for you and your sister, we can leave soon," prompted the policeman.

It didn't take Nora long to pack their few things. The policeman brought a box. "You can put your blankets and sheets in here. They can always use them at the orphanage. The boys are ready. I checked that they didn't leave anything, but you might check, too."

Nora looked around the bare, dreary room. Papa and Mama had covered the walls with pretty flowered paper and painted the woodwork. Now the paper was water-stained where the rain had leaked through the roof, and the woodwork was scratched and peeling.

Nora thought, "I'm sorry, Papa. Mama tried to keep us together and reminded us of our crowning glories, but it's been so long since she talked about them, I've nearly forgotten what they were. She rested her chin on her hand as she stared into the wavy mirror. "Let's see, Charley's was his...his...now I remember, his whistle. He could imitate any bird he heard. It's been a long time since I've heard Charley whistle. And Nils could grin wide enough for a whole watermelon slice to fit in his mouth, Papa used to say. It's been a long time since Nils grinned even a little grin."

"Miss, if you have everything, I think we should be going. Mother Superior hates to be kept waiting, and I promised her you would be there for the evening meal."

"Good-bye, little house, good-bye memories of Papa and Grandma," she whispered as she took one last look at the room. "I'm ready, sir," she said as she led Amanda out the door.

CHAPTER 3

Nora and the others were covered by buffalo robes as they traveled in the back of the policeman's wagon. Charley was shivering so badly Nora could hear his teeth chatter. She wrapped her arm around him.

"It's going to be okay, Charley, you'll see. In the spring, when Mama's well, she'll come and get us, and we'll all go home."

"We can't go home, Nora. Don't you remember Papa sold the house? By the time spring comes someone else will be living in it," cried Nils.

"We'll just find us another one, won't we, Nora?" asked Charley.

"Yes, we will, Charley. As long as Mama's there, I don't care where we live."

"How do we know Mama will even get well? What if she dies?" asked Nils.

"Mama isn't going to die, is she, Nora?" cried Amanda, tears in her eyes.

"Of course not, Amanda," said Nora, frowning at Nils.

"How do you know? You don't even know what's wrong with her, do you?"

"No, Nils, I don't, but I'm not going to be a 'Gloomy Gus' and frighten the little ones," she snarled at him.

The wagon stopped in front of a large brick building. Lamplights shone through many of the windows.

"Nora, I'm scared," said Charley.

"So am I, Charley. But it will be only for a little while before we're all together again. We'll get to eat together, and I'll tell you bedtime stories, just like at home. If we just do what they tell us, we'll be fine," assured Nora.

"Will you still kiss me good night every night?" asked Amanda.

"And I'll tuck Charley and Nils..."

"You ain't tucking me in. I'm almost as old as you and too big to be tucked in," said Nils, jumping down from the wagon and helping Charley and Amanda. Nora handed him the boxes and then remembered the basket Mrs. Florenz had given her.

"Oh, darn!" she exclaimed.

"What's the matter, miss?" asked the policeman.

"I just remembered I set a basket of food on the kitchen table when I came home and forgot it." She started to cry.

"Don't cry, miss. I'll get it and bring it here later. What's in it?"

"I don't know. Just some food Mrs. Florenz gave us when Amanda and I left her house. But if you bring it here, I have no way of returning the basket to her, and she is so proud of that basket. Her son made it for her before he died in the war. She trusted me with it, and now she will never trust me again. How can I get it back to her?"

"I'll go get it and return it to her when I make my rounds. So don't worry about it anymore. I'll take it to her and tell her where you are now living," promised the policeman. "But now let's get you in out of the cold."

"Thank you."

The children struggled up the walk against the cold north wind with their meager possessions. The police officer hurried ahead, opened the big doors, and escorted them inside.

Nora looked around in amazement. The room was huge and painted white. A stairway went upward until she couldn't see it anymore. Heavy, blue velvet drapes hung at the front windows. She could hear children laughing.

The police officer pulled on a heavy blue rope. Suddenly a woman appeared. She wore a long black gown, and her head was covered with a black shawl with her face surrounded by a stiff white board. A string of beads hung from her waist. Nora gasped and shrank back. The others gathered behind her.

Nora watched as the woman approached. "Good evening, Officer O'Herrity. Are these the children you told me about?" she asked.

"Yes, Sister. The oldest girl is Nora, the oldest boy is Nils, next is Charley, and the littlest tyke is Amanda. Children, this is Sister Mary Rose."

"Good evening, children. Thank you, officer. I'll take you to your rooms first. Then we will go to the dining room for supper," said the soft-spoken sister.

"Wait!" cried Nora running after Officer O'Herrity. "You didn't tell us where they took our mother."

The officer took Nora's hand in his. "Mother Superior will tell you all she can. I will go now to take care of that little matter we discussed about the basket, remember?"

"Yes, I remember. Thank you for all your help," she said shyly.

"Come, Nora, it's getting late. The girls will be wanting to clean up the kitchen," called Sister Mary Rose.

Nora hurried to join the group, and they ascended the stairs. On the second floor, the Sister stepped into a small bedroom with a bed, wash basin, a pitcher on a stand and a lamp and metal match holder. There was a row of nails on one wall. "You girls will sleep here tonight. Put your things down. Boys, you will sleep in the next room. Come, we will go to supper."

The dining room, like the front entrance, was immense, with many tables and benches. A half wall, with a wide shelf, divided the room from a brightly-lit kitchen where several older girls were laughing and talking while washing and drying dishes. Nora saw one of the girls clap her hands, and the other girls were almost instantly silent.

"Our newest children have arrived. Please serve them. Then, if you have finished your work, you may go to your rooms and study," said Sister Mary Rose as she motioned for the children to sit down.

Nora watched as two girls in white blouses and grey skirts entered the dining room with trays of food. A third girl carrying a tray with glasses of milk and silverware approached the table.

The first girl smiled and said, "Good evening, I'm Betsy."

"And I'm Janie."

Nora smiled at them and turned as Charley let out a squeal.

"Look, Nora, we each get two pieces of chicken!" he shouted.

Nora laughed. "We haven't had fried chicken in ever so long a time," she explained.

"Well, don't plan on it too often," said the girl handing out the glasses of milk. "We only get it when a farmer decides to cut down his chicken flock for the winter."

"Melanie!" exclaimed Sister Mary Rose.

"Sorry, Sister."

Nora watched as the girls filed by, bidding Sister Mary Rose good night.

Nora began eating her supper. Everything tasted so good! She looked up to see Charley watching her.

"Nora, can I have your other piece of chicken?" he asked.

Nora hesitated. Then she said, "Sure, Charley. I'm full anyway." She felt Sister Mary Rose's eyes on her and ducked her head while she finished her potatoes and peas.

Sister Mary Rose cleared her throat.

"If you have finished your meal, please bring your dishes to the kitchen. We'll wash them, and I will explain about the schedule. Tonight, you will sleep together in the rooms I showed you. In the morning you will hear bells ringing. The first set rings at 6:00. You will rise and dress for breakfast. After you have dressed, listen for the second set of bells. When you hear them, step into the halls and line up with the other children. You may sit together again here at this table. After breakfast, you will meet Mother Superior to be assigned to classrooms and then to the jobs you will be doing here."

Nora, who was holding Amanda on her lap, felt her stiffen. "You mean I have to work, too?" Amanda cried.

"Yes, even you, little one, will work. We all have to work or we can't stay here. Don't worry, it won't be hard," explained Sister Mary Rose.

Nora pulled Amanda close and smiled down at her.

Sister Mary Rose hung up the dish towel and motioned the children to follow her. They went up the stairs to their bedrooms.

"Good night, children. I'll see you at breakfast."

Nora and Amanda watched the boys go into their room, then went into theirs. Nightgowns were on their bed. Amanda snuggled the small one against herself, then tried it on.

"Look, Nora! It goes past my knees." Nora smiled and tried hers on. It fit comfortably. She curled up under the covers.

"Are you ready to hear a story?"

Amanda didn't answer; she was already asleep. Nora snuggled down beside her and slept.

The ringing of a bell and a gentle tap on the door woke Nora. A voice quietly said, "Good morning, I'm Beth. I served you dinner last night. I just wanted to be sure you woke up this morning on time."

Nora raised up to thank Beth, but the door closed, so she threw back the covers and lit the lamp on the dresser. She washed her face and hands and brushed her long hair before rebraiding it. Hanging on a nail, on the wall was a long-sleeved, white blouse and grey skirt like the girls in the kitchen wore. Nora dressed and then woke Amanda.

After Amanda was dressed and her hair was brushed into shining ringlets, the girls sat on their bed waiting for the second bell.

"Nora, did you bring my doll, Carrie?"

"Yes, it's in the box under the bed," replied Nora.

Amanda jumped down and began tugging everything out of the box.

"Stop, Amanda! I'll find her for you," scolded Nora.

"What is all this junk anyway?" asked Amanda.

"It's not junk. It's all we have left that was Mama's and Papa's. See, here is Mama's ruby brooch. If I had gotten to Mr. Claussen's with it yesterday, we wouldn't be here now. He wouldn't have told the policeman on us," said Nora angrily.

"Don't you like it here, Nora? I do. We don't have to go out in the cold to go to work. We have lots to eat and new clothes to wear. I like my new white blouse and blue skirt," exclaimed Amanda whirling around.

Nora watched her younger sister.

"What's the matter, Nora? Why aren't you happy?"

"I guess I just miss having Mama and the boys with us. But that will all change as soon as spring comes. And besides, we'll see the boys at breakfast, and nothing will keep us from being a family. Now," she said as she continued to straighten the things in the box, "here are letters Papa wrote to Mama while he was gone. And here's...was that the bell?"

Hurriedly she placed the items back in the box and slid it under the bed with the other box. Grabbing Amanda's hand, she hurried out the door to stop and stare. The hall was filled with children of all sizes finding places in line for breakfast. Nora turned as she heard the door behind her open and saw Nils and Charley. They were dressed in long-sleeved white shirts and dark trousers. Nils wore black and Charley had on blue. They came to stand beside Nora.

"Where do we fit in the line?" Nils whispered to Nora.

"I guess we just wait until the end comes and join in then," replied Nora.

"Good morning, children. I'm Sister Mary Cecilia. Come with me. Tomorrow you will be able to find your own way."

Nora and the children followed the new Sister to the dining room. She led them to the serving window where they were given trays filled with food. Charley grinned up at Nora. She smiled back at him.

"Hi, Nora. Remember me? I'm Beth."

Nora smiled at Beth. "Hi, thanks for waking us this morning. I had trouble remembering where I was when I woke up."

"Nora," explained Sister Mary Cecelia, "you and the children will sit here this morning. After you finish breakfast, return your trays to the window and then sit here until I come for you. You are to visit Mother Superior."

"Yes, Ma'am," replied Nora.

Nora watched the children as they finished their meal and carried their trays to the window Sister Mary Cecelia had pointed out. The silverware was placed in a pan of water, and the trays were stacked as each child passed. After all the children in the room had passed the window, Nora motioned for Nils, Charley, and Amanda to follow her. Amanda handed her tray to Nora. Nora started to take it.

"No, Nora, Amanda must learn to help herself."

Nora looked around to see Sister Mary Rose. "But she's too short to reach the top of the stack," replied Nora.

"Then she must learn to start a new stack. Amanda," said Sister Mary Rose sternly, "I'm sure a big girl like you can carry your own tray and start a new stack right here, can't you?"

Amanda looked up at the nun with tears in her big blue eyes and nodded. She placed the silverware in the water and set the tray on the counter. Nora smiled at her then stepped back to await her brothers.

"All finished, I see. Did you have enough to eat?" asked Sister Mary Cecilia.

"Oh, yes, Ma'am!" cried Charley.

"Good! Now sit down a minute before we go to see Mother Superior," suggested Sister Mary Cecilia. Nora and the youngsters sat down facing the Sister.

"When you speak to us you will say, 'Yes, Sister' or 'No, Sister,' not ma'am. You will address Mother Superior as 'Mother'. If you forget, don't worry; you'll all learn soon enough. Ready?"

Nora placed the children in front of her and, they followed Sister Mary Cecilia down the hall to a closed door. After knocking, they heard a voice call, "Come." Sister Mary Cecilia ushered the children in and introduced them to Mother Superior.

Nora watched the woman, who was dressed as the others, and wondered how she would ever learn to tell them apart.

"Nora, Officer O'Herrity said he didn't think you had been going to school because your mother has been ill for a long time. I guess we will put you in with the girls your age and go from there. Nils will go with the boys his age, as will Charley. Now as far as sleeping rooms, Amanda will go with Sister Mary Grace in the east wing with the three- to seven-year-olds. Charley, you'll go to the north wing with the eight- to eleven-year-olds. Nils, you will be in the south wing with twelve- to fifteen-year-olds. Is something wrong, Nora?"

Nora sat with her mouth wide open. Slowly she closed it, her eyes beginning to fill with tears, and said, "But Nils is only eleven. Won't he go with Charley?"

"According to his birth date, he will be twelve in a couple of months, so we really should just start him out there. It's less crowded. Besides, Charley needs to learn to be on his own. Now, Nora, you'll go on the second floor in the east wing. We will start you in the laundry. Sister Mary Pauline will show you what you are to do. Are there any questions?"

Nora sat still, tears streaming down her face. "Does this mean we won't be together as a family?" she asked.

"Nora, my dear, we are all a family, one big family."

"But I promised Mama I wouldn't let anything separate us," she cried.

"You will see each other from time to time. But you will be busy with your education and the work assigned to you."

"What about our mother? Where is she and how long will she have to stay there?" asked Nora, wiping her eyes with the hankie Mother Superior had given her.

"Officer O'Herrity stopped by this morning and said your mother has been transferred to a convalescent home for people with tuberculosis. He said she should be well enough to be released by mid-summer.

All she really needs is rest and good food. I'm sure when she is well enough, she will come to get you. In the meantime, you will be well cared for."

"But won't we get to stay together as a family?" Nora asked again.

"I'm sorry, Nora, but we just are not set up to handle individual families. Just try, and I know you will soon be happy as part of our whole family."

"Yes, Mother Superior," she replied. But, she thought, "We won't stay here. I won't let Amanda forget who she is. I won't let Nils and Charley become just one of the boys. We will be a family again. I promised Mama, and I plan to keep that promise, no matter what it takes."

CHAPTER
4

Several days later, Nora found Beth grinning at her through the steamy hot water rising from the laundry tub of white clothes she was running through the wringer.

"Hi, Beth, I thought you were on kitchen detail," she said.

"I was, but Myra is sick, so Sister Mary Katherine sent me down," explained Beth, her blue eyes sparkling. "How's it going, Nora? Are you getting settled? Where's that cute brother of yours?"

"You mean Charley? They put him in the shoe repair shop."

"Noooo, I mean Nils."

"Oh, Nils is out in the barn helping with the animals. Now that he has a nice warm coat, he really enjoys working outside."

"Where's Amanda?"

Nora's head drooped and tears started. "The last time I saw her, she was too busy playing dolls to talk."

"Nora, what's wrong?"

"Nothing. It's just...Oh, Beth, you seem so happy here. I try, but I'm just not. Nils loves to be outside, so I never see him. Charley whistles all the time, so I know he's happy. He's getting fat, too. He said Sister Mary Faustina scolded him because he gained so much weight she can't let his pants out anymore."

"Sister Mary Faustina is just teasing. She's always happy when she has to alter our clothing. It shows we're getting enough to eat." Beth swirled her stick in the tub, trying to catch an apron to run through the wringer.

"I know," replied Nora. "But he just doesn't need me. And Amanda! She told me to go away, she was too busy to talk to me." Tears ran down her cheeks.

Beth patted her shoulder. In the silence, Nora saw that Beth, too, was crying. "I'm sorry, Beth. I didn't mean to make you cry. It's just I promised Mama and Grandma we'd be a family no matter what. Our family, not a great big orphanage family," she cried angrily.

"But, Nora, we're a nice family. I've been here since I was three when Mama and Papa were killed in a carriage accident. I think it's nice here," protested Beth.

"Oh, Beth, it is nice here, really it is! But I've always helped care for Amanda and the boys. And I worry whether or not Mama will be well enough to care for us by next spring. Officer O'Herrity says she's not gaining her strength back as quickly as the doctors had hoped.

If we don't get back together as a family soon, Amanda and Charley won't remember her at all!"

"But didn't you once say that the important thing to remember is, 'you have a crowning glory and that is what makes you so special; you can do anything you have to?' Well, you still have your beautiful, almost-red hair," Beth said tugging at her mousy-colored hair. "And I've seen Nils grin and you're right, it is so wide you could fit a slice of watermelon in. Charley's whistle makes everyone smile. And Sister Mary Christina is teaching him to whistle the songs we sing. Did you ever tell me what Amanda's crowning glory is?" Beth swished the snowy white aprons in the cold rinse water.

Nora stared across the room. She remembered asking Grandma what Amanda's crowning glory was, and Grandma sighed and said, "Dear, I don't know anything about crowning glories anymore and I'm too tired to care." She died two days later.

"Nora?" prompted Beth.

"Girls, quit dawdling and hang that laundry!" scolded Sister Mary Pauline.

"Yes, Sister," they said.

Nora looked at the big clock on the wall. If she hurried, she might have time to catch one of the children at their job.

"Sister, Beth and I hung all the white clothes, and it's a few minutes till class time. May I run up to the kitchen to see Amanda?"

Sister Mary Pauline smiled and nodded.

"Thank you, Sister," said Nora. She rushed off to the kitchen.

"Hi, Amanda, are you about finished sorting the forks so we can talk?"

Amanda glanced around. "No," she said sadly. "I've got one big tray left. I forgot to come to work, and Sister Mary Rose said I must stay here alone and think about being a good helper."

"I'm sorry, Nora, but Amanda is being punished and can't have visitors," explained Sister Mary Rose.

"And then I promised Kathleen she could read me a story. She is a good reader. I can hardly wait 'til I can read and then I won't need anybody!" exclaimed Amanda.

Nora stumbled out of the kitchen. Amanda didn't need her! Charley and Nils didn't need her! She wiped her tears and knocked on Mother Superior's door. Sister Mary Ellen answered.

"May I help you?" she asked. "Mother Superior has a visitor."

"I need to talk to her. May I wait until the visitor leaves?"

"I'm not sure how much longer he will be. Won't you be late for class?"

"I'll watch the clock," she promised as she tiptoed into Mother Superior's room and seated herself in one of the big overstuffed chairs in the back of the room.

"It's settled then, Mother. We will start here in Albany with the Orphan Train and go as far west as Nebraska to find homes for the children before coming back to New York," said a deep voice.

Nora peeped over the chair back and saw a tall man in front of Mother Superior's desk.

"Yes," said Mother Superior. "I have had several replies to the bulletins I sent to our churches in the western states. Several families are interested in taking homeless children. Thank you for coming. Good day."

Nora watched the man walk past her. Maybe we could be sent to someone as a family, she thought. The clock began to strike and it reminded her of class time.

"Nora, is there something you need to talk about?" asked Mother Superior.

"Yes, Mother, but not right now. I have to go to class," she cried.

"I can write you a tardy slip if necessary."

"Thank you, but it can wait. I have to think about it some more, then I'll come to see you, I promise," said Nora, smiling broadly.

Nora slid into her desk just as the teacher closed the door.

"Nora, please go to the blackboard and add the column of figures. Nora. Nora?!"

"What? Oh, Sister, I'm sorry. I was thinking," cried Nora.

Her classmates laughed loudly. Nora laughed with them and hurried to the blackboard.

Later that evening, as the girls in Nora's dormitory settled down to sleep, a voice was heard from down the hall, "Lights out, girls. Settle down and go to sleep. That means no talking."

The girls responded with "Good night." Slowly they settled into their beds.

"Nora, be still!" whispered Beth. "That old bed squeaks when you move. That's why we made you trade with Sarah, cause you never move. Tonight you're noisier than Sarah ever was."

"Sorry, I just can't go to sleep. I'm thinking," whispered Nora.

"Well, lie still and think," whispered another, "or we'll all fall asleep in class tomorrow."

Nora smiled. The girls were all so nice here, but if she could get her family on the Orphan Train maybe they could find a home together. And maybe they could earn enough money to pay train fare for Mama to join them when she was well. She smiled, drew her legs up, and the bed squeaked.

"Nora!" came whispered shouts.

"Sorry." Nora lay still and said the night prayer she had learned as a child, but she fell asleep before she finished it.

"Good morning, Mother Superior. May I visit you today?" asked Nora from the bottom of the stairs in front of the chapel.

"Why, Nora! Child, rising time isn't for another half hour."

Nora saw Mother Superior glance at her nightgown and robe and then down at her bare feet.

"How long have you been standing there? Never mind. Come join me in my office."

"Thank you, Mother," she said.

She followed Mother Superior into the office where a fire roared in the fireplace. Mother Superior gave Nora a woolly blanket, then handed her a heavy mug.

"Don't worry," she said with a smile. "It's only warm milk. Now, what is so urgent that you're up in the middle of the night to talk to me?"

Nora glanced at the clock. It struck half past five.

"Yesterday, Mother, when I came to see you, I over-heard a man talking about an Orphan Train going as far as Nebraska. What did he mean?"

"Oh!" said Mother Superior. "You haven't been happy here have you, Nora?"

Nora looked down at her hands.

"It's all right child. I won't scold you for not trying harder to get used to us. So many children were home-less, abused, hungry, living in the streets, so they are content to be in a warm building. They have enough to eat, go to school, and some of them are happy because they are kept busy learning a trade.

But you, Nora, have a mother, can remember your father and grandmother. You also remember the promise you made to keep your family together. Now you see each of them happy and blending into our big family and you are afraid you can't keep your promise."

Nora looked up at the kind, loving face and smiled a little. "Yes, I'm afraid. I know in my heart my mother may never be well enough to leave the sanitarium. I don't want Amanda and Charley forgetting her, so last night I thought and thought about what that man said, and decided I'd ask you if anyone would take a family." She crossed her fingers and hid them in her lap.

Nora waited what seemed to be a long time before Mother Superior spoke. "Nora, there is a greater chance of your family being separated if you were to go on the Orphan Train. In Iowa, a family has asked for a five-year-old girl; in Oklahoma, I have a request for a ten- or eleven-year-old boy. Farmers always need strong, healthy boys and girls of twelve or thirteen. Once you're on the train, I have no control of where any child goes beyond the town marshal's and minister's assurance your new family is a good Christian family. So I can't promise your family would remain together."

Nora's shoulders drooped. She felt Mother Superior's hand on her shoulder. "I'm sorry, child. It would just be best if you accepted us here and made the best of it. But, Mr. Martin is returning in a few days; I will ask him if there is a chance a family of four can be accepted. In the meantime, try to be happy. Nils, Charley, and Amanda seem to be."

In the next few days, Nora tried to smile and be happy. She joined the girls who laughed and talked about boys and the styles of clothing they would wear when they no longer were required to wear uniforms. But at night, she cried silently for her lost dream.

Nora was scrubbing a pot some potatoes had been cooked in when she felt a hand on her shoulder. She looked into the face of Sister Mary Christine.

"Mother Superior wants to see you, Nora."

"Thank you, Sister."

"Nora, what did you do?" teased Beth.

"I bet she sneaked out to see Jack. I saw him wink at you, Nora," said Janet.

Nora smiled. "Go away, all of you. She probably wants to tell me she wants me back in the laundry because I'm the only one who can get her sheets and pillow cases as white and stiff as she likes it," she said handing the dishcloth to Beth.

Nora knocked lightly on Mother Superior's door. She waited, then knocked louder, the fingers of her left hand crossed.

"Come."

Nora stepped into the room. Mother Superior sat at her desk and Mr. Martin occupied a chair in front of it.

"Nora, this is Mr. Martin. We have discussed the possibility of a family going west and staying together. He thought if you had relatives living out west, maybe they would consider taking in four children. Do you know of any relatives?" she asked.

Nora's shoulders drooped once more. "I can't remember ever hearing of anyone, Mother, but I'll ask Nils," replied Nora, her hopes rising. "May I see you after talking to him?"

"Yes, of course."

Nora stepped out and closed the door, forgetting to thank Mr. Martin. She reopened the door and heard Mother Superior sigh, "That poor child is going to pine away if we don't help her. Her parents and grandmother made her promise to keep the family together. That was an impossible task, I feel. But I'll do all I can to keep her hopes up. Maybe something will come up to permit it. She hopes her mother will soon become well so they can go home, but the mother just isn't responding to treatment. And the children aren't allowed to visit her, so she hasn't any reason to try to get well." She sighed again. "I hope Nora doesn't live to regret her decision to go west, if she can work it out."

Nora knocked on the door.

"Come."

"I'm sorry, Mother, I got halfway up the stairs before I remembered my manners." She flashed Mr. Martin a smile and said, "Thank you, Sir, for the idea of relatives out west. Good-bye."

Walking slowly down the hall, she tried to remember anything Mama might have said about aunts or uncles, cousins, anybody they could live with.

"Hi, Nora. Are you sleepwalking?"

"No, Jack," she said, "I was thinking. Is Nils in from the barns?"

"Yes, he came in when I did."

"When you see him again, would tell him I need to see him right away, here, in the front hall?" she asked.

"Sure, Nora. How are things going?" he asked, but Nora was walking away from him pulling her heavy braid.

Nora paced up and down the hall. Where was Nils? What if Jack had forgotten or didn't go right to the boys' dormitory?

"Hi, Nora. Jack said you wanted to see me. I can't stay long, I have to study. Did you know I'm at the top of my class?"

"Never mind that now, Nils. Can you remember Mama ever talking about relatives that lived out west?"

"What? Nora, what are you talking about?"

"Mr. Martin said if we had relatives out west that would take us as a family, we could ride the Orphan Train taking orphans as far as Nebraska to find new homes. So, do you remember Mama talking about any aunts or uncles or cousins out west?" cried Nora.

Nils stared at her. "What do you mean, Orphan Train? We aren't orphans and we're all happy here except you. Why are you always trying to change things? Can't you just be happy here until Mama gets well? Then we can be a family again. Gotta go. See you around," said Nils, as he hurried down the hall.

"Nils," cried Nora, "you don't understand. Mama may never get well, and if she does, she could join us." Nora then realized she was talking to an empty hallway.

"Hi, Nora. Was that Nils you were talking to? I never see him very much since he works in the barns. I've heard he's really good with animals."

"Oh, Charley, I'm sorry. I just thought Nils could help me remember the names of any relatives who live out west so we could ride the Orphan Train and be a family again," cried Nora. "Do you remember ever hearing of any cousins, aunts, or uncles?"

"No," said Charley slowly, "and I don't know what an Orphan Train is, either. How would that make us a family again? Would Mama be well enough to ride the train, too?"

"Never mind, Charley," said Nora, as she slowly walked away.

"Nora, would there be any names in those letters Papa wrote to Mama when he was in the war? Or did you throw them away?"

Nora whirled around. "Charley, I love you. I have all the letters. I'll look through them now. Thanks. See you." She walked as quickly as she could without breaking the rule about running in the halls. She couldn't wait to read those letters. There had to be a name! She tugged at her braid and smiled a big smile. A family again; that would be so nice!

CHAPTER 5

Nora sat on her bed amidst envelopes and letters.

"Hi, Nora, what are you doing?"

"Oh, Beth, I'm trying to find a name of a relative," replied Nora, scanning the pages.

"Can I help?"

Nora looked up. "Well, I'm not sure. These are letters Papa wrote to Mama while he was in the War. I'm looking to see if he wrote about any relatives who live out west. I guess you could read them too."

Nora and Beth sat side by side, reading, being careful to put each letter in the right envelope when they were finished.

"Nora, would Nebraska be out west?"

"Nebraska? Yes, why?" asked Nora.

"Well, this letter says, 'I ran across a man whose sister is married to my cousin, Henley Fairacres. He had been shot in the leg, and I was able to save it from amputation though he will limp the rest of his life.'"

"Skip the details. Where does it say anything about Nebraska?" cried Nora looking over Beth's shoulder. Impatiently, she took the letter and read where Beth's finger pointed.

"'He said his sister and my cousin were homesteading at Pine Bluff, Nebraska. He thought, after the war, he might go out there to see about a homestead of his own."

"That's it! That's all I need!" cried Nora, her eyes flashing quickly as she gathered the other letters and stuffed them into her wicker suitcase, slid it under the bed, and ran from the room.

"Come."

Nora opened the door. "I found it, Mother, a letter that tells of Papa's cousin and wife who live in Nebraska. Will you write and ask them if we can live with them as a family, or should I?" she asked, her face shining with happiness.

"Now, Nora, you mustn't get your hopes up. What if they have a family or never wanted one?" cautioned Mother Superior. "I'll write to them and hope we hear from them soon."

"Thank you, Mother. And you will let me know as soon as you hear from them, won't you?"

"Yes, Nora, I promise I will let you know their answer one way or the other. But you must promise me something," replied Mother Superior.

"If I can," replied Nora, frowning.

"Promise me you will wear that beautiful smile you just smiled. We need to see more of it."

Nora wore her smile and greeted everyone happily day after day. Two weeks passed and still Mother Superior hadn't called her into her office about the letter. One day, as she was pacing back and forth in front of the office door, Sister Mary Rose stepped out.

"Why, Nora, I was just coming to find you. Mother Superior has a letter..."

Nora didn't wait to hear anymore. She darted through the door to Mother Superior's desk.

"You have a letter for me?" she cried breathlessly.

"Child, you're going to wear yourself out and me, too, running in the halls," said Mother Superior.

"But, I never run in the halls, Mother. I was waiting outside your door. What does the letter say?" Nora asked impatiently, leaning over Mother Superior's shoulder.

Mother Superior handed her the letter.

Nora read, "My husband and I have no children. We cannot afford to pay the train fare, and the children must work for their room and board."

"Oh," said Nora quietly.

"I know you were hoping to earn some money to pay your mother's way west when she was well enough to travel. But this changes things, doesn't it?" asked Mother Superior.

"Yes," replied Nora. "I need to think on it. Maybe the other letters have different relatives' names in them we could write to. Thank you, Mother."

Every spare minute Nora could find, she studied the remaining letters and reread the first ones. She sent a letter to her mama with Officer O'Herrity, but he wasn't able to visit with her and there was no answer from her.

Nora wandered outside where the younger children were playing in the spring sunlight. Amanda sat in the shade of an elm tree with a younger child. Nora watched as Amanda patted the crying child's shoulders.

"Don't cry, Jessica," Amanda said. "Being an orphan doesn't hurt after awhile. And it's nice here. We have lots of friends, food, and clean clothes. I know, you can be my little sister."

The child looked up at Amanda. "Are you an orphan, too?"

Amanda nodded. "Yes. I don't have anyone either."

Nora stomped over to Amanda and angrily grabbed her by the shoulder. "You are not an orphan!" she screamed. "You have a mother, brothers, and sister."

"Nora, don't," cried Amanda. "I can be an orphan 'cause I can't remember what Mama looks like. And I never see Nils or Charley."

Nora raced across the playground. She forgot the rule about no running in the halls and sprinted to Mother Superior's office to knock on the door.

"Come."

Nora entered and said, "Please write the letter to my father's cousin that we will be happy to come and be part of their family."

"Nora, are you sure? What about Nils, Charley, and Amanda? Do they want to go?" asked Mother Superior.

"It doesn't matter. I was left in charge, and you said if we had a family out west, we could ride the Orphan Train."

"Sit down, child, and tell me what happened."

Nora felt tears on her cheeks but didn't care. She let them fall while she told Mother Superior what Amanda had said about being an orphan and not remembering her mother and never seeing Charley or Nils. "At least if we go to relatives, we can be a family and talk together and plan things together and eat as a family..."

"Nora, Nora, I understand," said Mother Superior, holding Nora close to her. "I will write the letter and make train arrangements today."

Nora wiped her eyes and stepped back. "Thank you, Mother Superior. I'll tell Nils and Charley."

Nora crossed the playground to the barnyard where Nils was repairing a harness.

"Nils, I came to tell you Mother Superior is writing a letter to Papa's cousin in Nebraska to say we will be on the next Orphan Train."

Nils glared at her. "You have no right to decide if I'm going to Nebraska or anywhere else, Nora," he cried angrily. "Can't we just stay here, at least until Mama is well?"

"No, we are going west and we will be a family!" Nora stated firmly, turning her back on her brother.

Nils ran to join her. "I'll just ask Mother Superior if I have to go," he said.

Nils and Nora sat in Mother Superior's office.

"Nils, I know you have adjusted and are happy here, but Nora isn't. And you do have family in Nebraska that has invited you to live with them. They are farmers and, no doubt you will be expected to help with the animals," comforted Mother Superior. "The next Orphan Train leaves in two weeks, so you will be in time for spring planting. Nora, we must gather clothing and bedding to send with you. I have written to tell them when to expect you. May you find the happiness you so desperately seek," she said.

Nora smiled constantly. Her dream was coming true, so it was easy to smile. She asked permission to visit her mother to explain about going west, but the doctors said no because she wasn't strong enough to take the news just yet.

"Hi, Nora. Guess what! I'm going to Nebraska, too," said Beth. "We'll be traveling together until we get to a place called Omaha. Isn't that exciting?"

The girls worked side by side planning their trip west and the possibility of visiting each other once they arrived at their new homes.

Nora saw less of Nils than before, and the few times she did see him, he glared at her and turned away quickly before she could speak.

She talked to Charley, but didn't hear him whistle anymore. When she asked him if he was happy about going west, he just shrugged and went his way.

"Amanda, aren't you excited about going on a long train ride?" she asked.

"No, I don't want to go. I'm happy here where my friends are."

"Never mind, you'll soon make new friends," said Nora. "So will Nils and Charley, and we'll all be one family again. If only Mama would get well," she said, tugging at her braid.

The train that would transport thirty children to new homes in the west stood at the station. Mother Superior had come down to bid them all good-bye.

"If ever you need me, just write and I'll try to help you," she promised as she hugged Nora.

Nora smiled and nodded. She breathed deeply. The day had finally arrived and it was beautiful. The sun was shining, and the scent of apple blossoms filled the air. Thirty children and their baskets, bundles, and suitcases filled the train depot. Three adults assigned to the group were trying to sort everyone out and get them on the train before the conductor yelled, "All aboard."

Finally, everyone was settled into the passenger car. Children huddled together, fearing yet another new world. Nora sat up brightly and looked around. She saw Nils in a far corner and smiled at him. He scowled and turned his head.

"Aren't you afraid?" asked Beth. "What if my new family doesn't like me? I'm not pretty, you know."

"All you have to do is listen, learn what they want from you and do it. Being pretty has nothing to do with it. I plan to help Aunt Augusta all I can. We'll get along just fine, I'm sure. Uncle Henley will be glad Nils is so good with animals. Charley and Amanda will hear my stories about Mama and Papa, and we will be a family again," Nora explained triumphantly.

The days and miles passed. Nearly every day, Nora said good-bye to some of the children and watched as they became members of new families.

In Omaha, Nora hugged Beth. "Oh, Beth, I'm going to miss you so much! But we'll write to each other and maybe we'll even get to visit if our family ever comes to Omaha."

"Or mine to Pine Bluff. Good-bye, Nora, be happy!" cried Beth.

Two days after leaving Omaha, Nora heard the conductor calling, "Pine Bluff, all out at Pine Bluff."

POOR AS CHURCH MICE

Nora gathered up her wicker suitcase and moved to the aisle to awaken Nils and the others. She needed help gathering their bundles of blankets, towels, and other items Mother Superior had sent with them. Aunt Augusta had written she had no bed linens or towels or washcloths to spare and felt the children should supply their own.

Struggling with all her bundles, Nora suddenly thought, what if Aunt Augusta doesn't want us or she was only doing it out of charity?

"Come along, miss. We have a schedule to keep," said the conductor, helping her balance herself.

"Nils, come help me," she said as she passed his seat.

He just grumbled. The conductor pulled him up by his collar and handed him a load. Amanda grabbed Nora's skirt and stood crying. Charley waited to be told what to do. Slowly, Nora got her family out of the train and onto the platform. No one was waiting for them.

Nora said to the conductor, "This is Pine Bluff, Nebraska, isn't it?"

"Yes, Miss. good-bye and good luck with your new family."

"But no one is here. Can't you wait until someone comes to get us?"

"No, miss."

"Oh, wait, please wait."

"Here comes a wagon now. Good-bye."

"Good-bye, good-bye," called the children from the train as it pulled out of the station.

Nora watched the team of horses and the rickety wagon coming toward them. "Please, please, let that be Aunt Augusta," she whispered. She repeated it over and over, her crossed fingers hidden in her skirt.

"Hello," called the man driving the horses. "Are you the Tucker children?" He pulled the reins, bringing the team to a halt.

"Oh, yes, yes, we are. Are you Aunt Augusta and Uncle Henley?" Nora called as a short, slender man climbed down from the wagon and walked toward them.

"If you are the Tuckers, I'm your father's cousin, Henley Fairacres."

Nora noticed his bib overalls and blue chambray shirt were clean, but badly frayed. His straw hat dipped and flopped as he walked.

"Is this your plunder?" he asked.

Nora motioned for the children to gather their belongings. Uncle Henley lifted everything into the wagon and then the girls. The boys climbed in by themselves.

Nora looked at the woman on the seat. She had not spoken or turned around to greet them. Nora stood directly behind the unmoving woman. Finally, she cleared her throat. The woman still didn't move.

"Hello, I'm Nora Tucker and these are my brothers, Charley and Nils. And this is my sister Amanda. We're happy to be..."

"Sit down. We have a long way to go," said the woman without turning her head.

Nora sat on her bundle. She didn't dare look at Nils for tears had sprung to her eyes.

He tugged at her skirt and whispered, "I told you so."

The road they followed was nothing more than a path in the vast prairie of green grass. There were no trees, but wildflowers colored the land and nodded as the wagon passed. Nora's back began to ache for there was nowhere to rest it. Amanda bounced and whimpered. Nora motioned for her to be quiet. Nils glared at Nora and then looked away. Had Mother Superior been right? Was it possible she had made a mistake? Suddenly, she heard a bird whistle, then an echo. Charley was leaning against the tailgate repeating the bird's call. Nora smiled, Charley was happy. Maybe that was a good sign, and everything would be alright.

Another hour passed before they saw any buildings. A ramshackle wooden house and barn appeared on the horizon. The corral around the barn had broken rails. Chickens scratched everywhere on the bare ground, and a big shaggy dog ran barking toward the wagon.

"Whoa, whoa," called Uncle Henley pulling on the reins.

The wagon stopped, and Uncle Henley climbed down. "Come on, young'uns. Carry your belongins in, and Aunt Augusta will show you where you'll sleep. Then git yourselves back out here to carry these vittles in."

"And be quick about it. No dawdling," called Aunt Augusta.

"Yes, Ma'am," replied Nora, hurrying the children to the house with their boxes and bundles.

Nora and the others stopped just inside the door of the kitchen. A ladder in the middle of the room led up to a hole in the ceiling.

"Where are the bedrooms?" she asked.

"Right up that ladder," replied her aunt.

Nora raised her eyes, then glanced at Aunt Augusta.

"Don't just stand there, Girl, hurry up! There are boxes to be brought in from the wagon. And you, boy, you go help your uncle after you carry your things upstairs."

Nora grabbed a box, balanced it on her shoulder, and started up the ladder. Nils and Charley soon followed.

Amanda stood at the bottom of the ladder. "I'm scared," she howled.

"Nils," whispered Nora, "go down and get Amanda."

Nils glared at her. "You go, it was your idea to come out here to live."

"Girl, get down here as soon as you make them beds. I left sheets and quilts. I'll just take the ones the orphanage sent with you for our bed since I gave you ours," called Aunt Augusta.

Nora looked at the shabby worn quilts and gritted her teeth. Then she heard Aunt Augusta say to Amanda, "Come on, little one, we'll go make my bed with these poor blankets you brought."

Nora started toward the hole with the ladder. Nils grabbed her, she whirled on him her eyes flashing. "Those blankets are much better..."

"Look, Nora, forget about that. We are here and here we stay."

Nora dropped her eyes. Nils was right. She had gotten them here, and they were going to have to make the best of it.

"All right," she whispered, sitting on her bed.

The mattress rustled. She felt it. It felt like the cornhusks on the corncobs she used in the stove at the orphanage to heat the water for laundry and dishes.

"Nora, we got to go. She'll be hollering up here again," warned Nils.

Nora looked at him and Charley. "I know this isn't what we had hoped for, but at least we are a family again. Soon we will be laughing and talking and really enjoying ourselves."

"Yeah, I can just hear Aunt Augusta laughing. Can't you Charley?" Nils asked sourly.

"Girl, you and those young'uns git down here and git that wagon unloaded!" yelled Aunt August from the bottom of the ladder.

CHAPTER
6

Nora turned in her bed. The corn husks rustled. She snuggled farther down under the quilt, hoping to go back to sleep.

"Girl, Girl, get up. It's wash day."

Nora groaned and rolled over. Slowly, she sat up, her back aching from sleeping on the thin cornhusk mattress. Uncle Henley had promised her more husks for her mattress as soon as the corn crop was harvested this fall.

Slowly she yawned and dressed. Aunt Augusta stood at the bottom of the ladder with water pails. She thrust them at Nora.

Nora, barefooted, started out the door. "Should've put your shoes on, Girl. Last night was the first frost," cackled Aunt Augusta. "Never mind, you're started now, go ahead. You can put them on for the next trip."

Nora slowly and carefully stepped on the frosty, cold ground until she heard Aunt August snicker again. Then she walked firmly and quickly to the yard pump. Grabbing the hem of her skirt, she wrapped it around the metal handle and began pumping.

Slowly, she made her way back to the house, careful not to splash the cold water on her bare feet.

After pouring the water into the reservoir of the big, black cookstove, Nora went up the ladder and dried her feet with her quilt before drawing on her heavy woolen socks and shoes.

She shook the boys awake. Nils flashed his grin at her.

"What are you so happy about?" she asked angrily.

"Today Uncle Henley is going to Shelsburg to see about sellin' our corn crop. Just give me some frosts, and we'll be a harvestin'!" he sang.

"Humph," snorted Nora.

"Nils, will you ask Uncle if I can go, too?" asked Charley.

"I'm sorry, Charley, but Uncle said Aunt Augusta needed you to gather wood to heat for the washin'."

"Nils, the words have a 'g' on the end of them. Washing, I-n-g, ing. Harvesting, not harvestin'," scolded Nora.

"You aren't happy here either are you, Nora? You know, when you first talked about coming here, I was so mad at you, but now I love it. Uncle Henley has taught me so much. He says if I ever got lost, he wouldn't worry 'cause I could take care of myself," bragged Nils.

"Girl, git down here and git breakfast started," bellowed Aunt Augusta.

"You better get up. Breakfast will be ready in a few minutes," she told the boys.

"Girl!!"

"I'm coming as soon as I braid my hair," called Nora through gritted teeth.

"Forget that hair and git down here, now!"

Nora pulled her hair away from her face into a knot on the top of her head and held it in place with three large hairpins. Tendrils slipped out of the bun and curled against her thin drawn face. She heard a hairpin hit the linoleum when she stepped off the ladder. By the time she had the oatmeal dished up, all three pins had fallen out and her hair cascaded down her back. She brushed her hand against her hair as she set the oatmeal on the table.

Uncle Henley smiled. "I like your hair like that, Nora. It makes you look like a young lady. You sure have pretty hair."

"Thank you, Uncle," she replied. Glancing at her aunt, she saw her touch her thinning gray hair. Straggles hung down around her face from the small bun at the back of her head.

As the day wore on, Nora became more and more angry. Nothing she did was right as far as Aunt

Augusta was concerned. Nora felt the braid she had quickly made earlier hang loosely down her back as she mopped the floor, and wished she dared go to her room and rebraid it. But after the numerous scoldings she had gotten so far today, she really didn't want to take any more chances.

Carrying the bucket of scrub water outside where she could dump it, she stared across the prairie. She had been wrong to make them come west. They weren't a family here anymore than at the orphanage. They didn't even all sit together at meals. Nora was usually kept busy serving after she cooked. Nils and Uncle Henley talked about the work they had done and what had to be done the next day. Amanda and Aunt Augusta played silly games at the table, and poor Charley was always so tired he had trouble staying awake.

Well, no matter. As soon as spring came, they were leaving. Nils had been all over the countryside with Uncle Henley, so he knew where the towns were located. If they could get away from Uncle Henley and Aunt Augusta when the weather was good for traveling on foot, they would pack up and go to a town. She was sure she could find work for both boys as well as herself, and maybe they, like Mrs. Florenz in New York City, would let her keep Amanda with her. Staring off into the future, she played with her braid.

"Girl, I'm tired of yelling at you. Answer when I speak!"

Nora looked up. Her aunt was glaring at her. "You just can't seem to keep your hands off the 'pretty hair,' can you? Well, we will just see how pretty it is when I git through with it!" Aunt Augusta trotted toward the barn.

Nora carried her bucket into the house and hung it on a nail. She watched for Aunt Augusta. Not seeing her, she started up the ladder. Suddenly she was grabbed from behind and slammed down on a kitchen chair. Aunt Augusta held her down and yelled for Charley. Nora fought against her aunt, but didn't have enough strength to get free.

"Sit on her, boy," screamed Aunt Augusta.

Charley just stared at Nora, his mouth open and tears streaming down his face. When he didn't move, Aunt Augusta grabbed him and slammed him down on Nora's legs. Nora found herself squeezed between the back of the chair and Charley. Aunt Augusta stood behind the chair and raised a pair of sheep-shearing scissors. Nora saw Charley's eyes widen as he screamed in her ear.

"Please, Aunt Augusta, don't kill Nora! She'll be good, I promise."

"Shut up, boy. Hold still, Girl, or I might snip your ear instead of your hair."

Nora felt a tug of her braid. "No!" she screamed. She saw Aunt Augusta swing a severed braid and toss it into the stove. Nora closed her eyes and reached up to feel the blunt, spikey strands of hair rubbing against her neck.

She opened them when she heard Amanda ask, "What are you doing, Auntie?"

"I just got rid of that 'pretty hair,'" she snorted.

"No, no," sobbed Nora. She felt Charley sag against her, his tears wetting the front of her dress.

"Now, Girl, maybe we'll get some work done around here. You won't have to spend so much time taking care of your 'pretty hair.' Now git out and gather them clothes off the line. Boy, you git some more wood from the woodpile. Come, Arielle, we'll go cut out some paper dolls from that magazine Uncle brought home last month," said Aunt Augusta taking Amanda by the hand.

"Her name is Amanda!" screamed Nora.

Aunt Augusta turned and said smugly to Charley, "We'll see about that. Git out to that woodpile. Arielle and I are goin' into the sittin' room, and we need some wood for the heatin' stove."

Nora nodded at Charley. He ducked his head, tears running down his face.

"I'm sorry about your hair, Nora," he whispered as he passed her.

Nora lifted her hand to her head and dropped it. Her eyes fell on the sheep shears lying on the floor where Aunt Augusta had dropped them. She stooped to pick them up, but Charley reached them first.

POOR AS CHURCH MICE

The parlor door opened, and Aunt Augusta stepped into the kitchen. "Ain't you gone for that wood yet?" she asked the boy, her eyes piercing his. She started toward him, her hand uplifted.

Nora saw him raise the sheep shears. "No!" she screamed and headed him out the doorway. She followed him and turned him toward the barn to put the shears away. After she had loaded his arms with wood for the stove, she went to the clothesline. After gathering the clothing, she entered the kitchen to see that Charley had tracked up her clean floor. She laid the armload of clean laundry on the table and got out the mop.

Swishing it over the worn and cracked linoleum, she remembered the marble floors at the orphanage in New York City. Tears fell as she gingerly touched the jagged edges of her hair.

"My crowning glory. I've lost my crowning glory."

When Nora served supper to the family, she saw the sadness in Uncle Henley's eyes as he looked at her raggedy, jaggedy cut hair.

"Don't worry, Nora, it will grow back soon and be as pretty as ever. Your Aunt Augusta said she tried to git the head lice out, but decided it was best to cut it off," he sympathized.

Nora's mouth dropped open. Nils looked at her and shook his head ever so little. Nora snapped her mouth shut and sat down to eat.

Nora woke up to a strange voice that night coming up through the floor grate. She lay down on the floor and saw Uncle Henley in the lamplight so she knew it was still night.

Shivering, she pulled the quilt off her bed and wrapped it around herself and lay back down on the floor.

She heard the strange voice speak again, "I don't know how long I'll stay. I've been working my way across the country since I was released from the army. Felt a need to come west and start life over. I had planned to stay here and work for you, but if you have your cousin's children, I'm sure you won't have enough work for me, too."

"Don't worry, Thomas, you stay, and we'll find a way for you to earn your living," Aunt Augusta promised.

"Augusta, we can't hardly feed the children with what we earn on this farm. We can't take anyone else to live and work here," cried Uncle Henley.

"Shut your mouth, Henley. He's family. He can do the work of both the boys and still help me in the house. Don't worry, Thomas. Just go to bed, and we'll work it out in the morning."

"Augusta, you know we can't feed five people besides ourselves. He can stay until he can find work on a nearby farm."

"Don't you worry about it, Henley. I'll ship those three older kids off to the orphanage because my brother is stayin' here, he and Arielle."

"Augusta!" shouted Uncle Henley. "Her name is Amanda. Our Arielle died ten years ago. We are not sendin' those children anywhere. We promised to take care of them."

"You, Henley, you promised to take care of them. I only promised they could live here and help with the work. Well, now we don't need them. We have Thomas. And it's a good thing, too. That youngest boy is sick most of the time. Seems he's always got the croup."

Nora wrapped the quilt tighter around herself. Aunt Augusta sounded as if she meant what she said about sending them to the orphanage. What could she do? Would Mother Superior take them back? Nora shivered.

CHAPTER
7

Nora climbed down the ladder the following morning and saw a tall, slender man sitting at the table drinking coffee. Aunt Augusta stalked out of her bedroom door.

"About time you got up," she snarled at Nora. "Poor Thomas had to make his own coffee, I see."

"Augusta, don't badger the girl. I'm quite capable of making my own coffee," replied the man.

"It makes no difference. She's here to work and she better git used to the idea. 'Course, who knows how long that will be," Aunt Augusta laughed behind her hand.

"Well, don't just stand there, Girl. Git the oatmeal cooked. Your uncle will be in soon wanting his breakfast. Sure turned cold in the night." She wrapped her work roughened hand around the cup of coffee Nora had poured. "That one is Nora. She's the oldest of the bunch of kids I was telling you about last night." She whirled toward the stove where Nora stood stirring the oatmeal. "That should be cooked enough by now," she snarled.

Nora lifted the heavy pot and started to the table. She was surprised when she felt the weight of the pan lifted from her hands. The stranger had lifted it from her and set it on the table. Nora quickly placed hot pads down and reset the hot, heavy pan. The man then walked down the length of the table Nora had set the night before when she had washed the dishes. Nora noticed the man limped when he walked and remembered what she had read in the letter, "I was able to save the leg, but he will walk with a limp the rest of his life."

"Excuse me, sir, but do you remember the doctor who operated on your leg?" she asked.

"Never you mind, Girl. It's too painful for Thomas to remember them days. He don't want to talk about them. Go on about your chores and don't bother him again," scolded Aunt Augusta.

Nora and the others were told to call the stranger Uncle Thomas. He smiled and helped them with their chores. One day, while Nora and Uncle Thomas were in the barn milking, Nora looked carefully around, then asked, "Sir, do you remember the man who operated on your leg?"

"I'll never forget him. He was truly concerned about saving it. The other doctors would have cut it off and moved on to the next wounded soldier. But he refused to give up on me. Why do you ask?" asked Uncle Thomas.

"He was our father. He died in the war. In one of his letters to Mama he wrote about you. He also wrote about Aunt Augusta and Uncle Henley living in Nebraska. It was where I got the idea we could live with them as a family and maybe bring Mama out to join us when she got..."

"Girl, haven't you finished milking that cow yet?" yelled Aunt Augusta from the barn door. It was after this Nora noticed Uncle Thomas had stopped smiling and left the house when Aunt Augusta scolded or screamed at them. One day, she heard Uncle Thomas tell Aunt Augusta not to be so hateful.

"Mind your own business, Thomas," Aunt Augusta snapped. "But it don't make no never mind, 'cause those three older ones are goin' to be hauled into the home for orphans jest as soon as I can get Henley to take me to town to sign the papers making them wards of the state."

Nora grabbed a shelf for support. Through a fog she heard Aunt Augusta say, "Where did that girl git to? Girl! Girl!"

Nora waited until she heard the screen door slam, then ran up to the attic. She lay on her bed, her head pounding.

When she heard Aunt Augusta come into the house, Nora went quickly downstairs and began peeling potatoes for supper.

That night, Nora wrapped herself in her quilt and lay on the attic floor in case Aunt Augusta and Uncle Henley decided to sit at the kitchen table and talk.

Uncle Thomas was given the bedroom Amanda had been using, and Amanda slept on a cot in Aunt Augusta and Uncle Henley's room.

Later, Nora woke up cold and cramped, so she crawled into bed. But every night after that she slept on the floor close to the floor grate. She tried to talk to Nils about it, but he said she was having bad dreams. He said he and Uncle Henley were discussing the spring crops they were planning on planting in a few months.

Then one night, loud voices woke Nora. Holding her breath, she listened.

"I told you, Henley, we are goin' to town this week. The judge will be there, and we'll git them papers drawn up for Arielle's adoption."

"Her name is Amanda!" shouted Uncle Henley. "Arielle died!"

"Sh! Don't wake those young'uns," whispered Aunt Augusta. "We'll change her name to Arielle, and she will be our own little girl. And then we'll get papers to have those other three put in the orphans' home. Now that Thomas is here and settled, he can be our hired hand."

"Augusta..." began Uncle Henley, but Nora knew the discussion was over. She had to make plans. They would have to leave now, in the middle of the winter, not in the spring as she had planned.

In the morning, Nora searched the pantry. She found jars of canned beef, strips of dried beef, and a hunk of hard cheese. In the cellar were potatoes and carrots. When she baked bread, she mixed up larger batches of dough, making extra loaves which she hid in an unused crock.

When she folded the laundry, she stuffed the warmest clothing in a box.

"Nora, I can't find my new wool socks," complained Nils.

"They're in the mending basket," replied Nora.

"Mendin' basket? Uncle Henley just bought them for me."

"Yes, and if Aunt Augusta finds out she'll bawl him out. So just put on your old ones, and I will get the new ones back as soon as I can," replied Nora.

Later that night, she saw the lamplight glare through the grate and woke Nils.

"I told Thomas today, Henley, that we're goin' to the county seat and signin' the papers for Amanda's adoption and for the other young'uns to go to the orphanage," Aunt Augusta's voice floated up from the kitchen.

Nora poked Nils, but he was awake.

"No!" said Uncle Henley.

"Yes," replied Aunt Augusta. "We're going, and we're taking Amanda!"

"Augusta, it is a twenty-five mile trip. Amanda won't be able to stand the cold that long," declared Uncle Henley.

"What about me? I get cold, too," Aunt Augusta whined.

"Good, we'll stay home," said Uncle Henley, pushing his chair back.

"No, we're going. We'll leave the girl here."

Nora looked at Nils. His eyes were large, his mouth hung open.

"We've got to go tomorrow," whispered Nora. "That way we'll have a two-day head start."

Nils nodded.

"What about food and blankets? Where can we go? Amanda can't walk very far," whispered Nils.

Nora sat at the foot of the boys' bed. "Nils," she whispered.

"Yeah?" answered Nils.

"I'm sorry I got us into this mess. I just wanted to be a family."

"I know. I liked living here and I thought Uncle Henley liked me. What about Uncle Thomas? How will we get away without him seeing us?" asked Nils.

"I don't know unless he stays in bed because his leg hurts. He does that sometimes, you know."

"Yeah, but where will we go?" asked Nils.

"Well, Aunt Augusta said they were going to the county seat. Where's that?"

"Lincoln. It's almost straight east," explained Nils.

"Then we'll go south," decided Nora.

"No, south of here isn't well settled. We might need help."

"We'd better stick to the roads so they can't follow our tracks," whispered Charley.

"Charley, why aren't you asleep? He's right, Nils."

"Yeah, but what do we tell people? Four kids with bundles walking in the middle of nowhere in the middle of winter."

"Well, nobody really knows us since Aunt Augusta and Uncle Henley never have visitors or go visiting. Except you, Nils. Some of the farmers might recognize you."

"We could tell them we are going to Omaha to meet Mama, and our aunt and uncle are sick with influenza..."

And since Mama doesn't know how to get to us, we are going to Omaha to meet her," continued Nora. "Which direction is Omaha?"

"Uh, northeast of here, I think. But what about food?" asked Nils.

"I have some loaves of bread, and we can take a jar or two of canned beef. There's a ham, and a chunk of cheese," said Nora. "Oh, oh," she pointed to the lamplight that suddenly appeared through the cracks in the attic floor where the door opened. She slid off the boys' bed and crept to hers, pretending to be going to sleep, hoping the boys did the same. Through half-closed eyes, she watched the feeble light rise, then fall and disappear. She rolled over, closed her eyes, and fell asleep saying her prayers.

Nora woke to bright sunlight peeping through the snow encrusted window. She jumped out of bed. Nils and Charley were still sleeping. She wrapped her quilt around herself and backed down the ladder. On the kitchen table were dirty dishes and a cold coffee pot. Sticking out from under the coffee pot was a ragged piece of paper. Nora pulled the paper out, it tore. She held it together and read it.

"Nils, come! Uncle Thomas has gone, too. He left a note for Aunt Augusta."

"What time is it?"

"I heard the clock in Aunt Augusta's room strike nine times when I came down the ladder," replied Nora.

"Nora," called Amanda, "I'm hungry."

"Then come out, and I'll fix you some oatmeal," said Nora.

"Auntie always carries me so my feet won't get cold," protested Amanda.

"Aunt Augusta went on a trip, and we're going on one, too."

Nora handed Nils the note. "Read it while I fix the last of the oatmeal," she told him.

"'Dear Sister,'" Nils read, "'I'm leaving. Don't hate the children so. Will settle in California. Brother Thomas.'"

"He's right, she was hateful, but Uncle Henley was nice. Nora, since Uncle Thomas left, can't we stay? Uncle Henley will need my help," begged Nils.

"No! We're going," stated Nora, scraping the last of the oatmeal into a bowl.

"But where? Amanda can't walk very far, and Charley just got over his cold. He's not well enough."

Nora tugged at her short spiky hair, remembering Aunt Augusta's hateful manner. "We are going," she replied. "We'll go to Omaha, and maybe the family my friend Beth lives with will help us."

Nora gathered all the sacks and bags while the boys did chores. She was slowly sorting them out when she heard Charley calling.

"Nora! Nora! Come see what I found."

She stepped out the door to see Charley pulling a sled. "Charley, that's perfect!" she cried as she placed the bags on it.

"Nils, did Uncle Henley keep any matches in the barn? I can only find three in the matchbox," Nora said.

"No," Nils replied as he tied a rope around the bundles. Nora placed the blankets they brought from the orphanage on the sled and had Amanda sit on them.

"Sit still while I check the house to see if we left anything," Nora told her.

She opened the door to find Nils at the table with the note from Uncle Thomas in his hand. "Look, Nora, if I just tear the rest of this off it sounds like Uncle Thomas took us with him. 'Dear Sister, I am leaving the children. Will settle in California. Brother Thomas." And if I erase 'Don't' and print in 'with,' put the period after 'children,' capitalize 's' on 'so,' it reads, 'Dear Sister, I am leaving with the children. So will settle in California. Your Brother Thomas.'"

Nora nodded. She knew it was wrong to tamper with other people's mail, but today she didn't care. "I don't care what you do, Nils. Let's go."

She settled Amanda in the sled, broke a cedar branch from the tree beside the barn and dragged it over the sled tracks and footprints. Nils began pulling the sled. They reached the road and their tracks mingled with horse and sleigh tracks Uncle Henley had made earlier that morning.

Nora and Nils took turns pulling the sled. The motion and bright snow made Amanda sleep. Charley walked alongside the sled. At noon, Nils pointed to a stand of trees and pulled the sled to them. Nora swept out their prints then unpacked the bread, meat, and cheese for sandwiches. After a short rest, they packed up and moved back to the road. Late afternoon, a jingling of sleigh bells brought the children up short. They pulled the sled off to the side of the road to let the horse-drawn sleigh pass.

"Whoa, whoa," commanded a deep voice. Nora saw Nils raise his hand and shook her head, but it was too late. The driver had stopped his team and stared down at them.

"Hello," she said.

"Hello, little lady. Where in the world are you children going on such a cold day as this?" he asked.

"We got word our mother arrived by train in Omaha, so we are going to meet her."

Dear Sister
I am leaving Don't Hate
the Children so Will settle somewhere
in California.
Yr Brother
Thomas

Dear Sister
I am leaving with
the children. So will settle
in California
Yr Brother
Thomas

"That's quite a walk. Couldn't your uncle take you?"

"He's sick," Nora replied quickly.

"Sorry to hear that about Henley," replied the man.

Nora frowned. "We better get moving. We need to find a place to spend the night," she said.

"Say, why don't I give you a ride to my old homestead. You could spend the night there."

Nora saw Nils smile. Before she could stop him he said, "Gee, thanks Mr. Jones, that would be swell." He lifted the sled into the sleigh. Rather than cause trouble, Nora helped him, then lifted Amanda in. When they were all settled, the sleigh started.

Nestled together, they slept. Nora felt the sleigh stop and woke to find it was dark. She climbed down and followed Mr. Jones into a sod house. He lit a kerosene lamp. It showed a dusty room with a fireplace, table, and benches, and in two corners were stretched rawhide strips for bed frames. On top of these were dusty buffalo robes. Nora frowned as she looked around.

"Sorry it isn't cleaner, Miss, but the Mrs. doesn't come out anymore, and the men who keep it aren't much for sweeping and dusting," apologized the man.

Nora smiled at him. "It is just fine," she answered, pulling her stocking cap off. She saw the man's eyes narrow as he glanced at her shaggy haircut. She ducked her head.

The man turned away. "There's plenty of wood, Miss. Have Nils haul in all you need. Soddies stay warm once they get warm, so build a good-sized fire and let it burn down, and you should be very comfortable."

"Thank you, again, Sir. You have been very kind. If you should see the sheriff..."

"Don't worry, Miss. He and I seldom cross paths. Good night, and good luck on your trip."

Nora watched the man leave and sent Nils to gather wood from the woodpile. Then she shook the buffalo robes outside.

After a hot meal, they sat around the fire. "How far do you think we've come, Nils?" asked Nora.

"The man said this soddy is about ten miles from Uncle Henley's and thirty miles from Omaha," replied Nils.

Nora bowed her head. How would they ever make thirty miles on foot before Uncle came looking for them?

"Don't worry, Nora, remember Uncle Thomas' note? He said he was going to California, and I made it look like he was taking us with him," comforted Nils.

"I know Nils, I just worry about Charley and Amanda. But, it's too late to turn back now. I guess I had better wash these dishes and get them packed for tomorrow. Where are Charley and Amanda?" she asked.

"Charley went up to the attic, and Amanda is on the bed telling the doll how mean we are to take her from Aunt Augusta."

Nora, weary from the long walk and ride, made them go to bed. The shaken buffalo robes over the rawhide frames were more comfortable than the corn husk mattresses and not so noisy. Everyone was soon asleep.

Suddenly, the door flew open, and Nora woke to a lantern swinging in her face. She sat up.

"Uncle?" she whispered.

But seeing a huge man behind the lantern, she knew it wasn't her uncle. "Who are you and what do you want?" she demanded.

The man moved closer, and she saw several other men hovering in the doorway.

"Uh, oh, miss, sorry to disturb your sleep, but we're looking for a runaway slave," explained the large man.

Whirling the lantern around, the man peered into each face. "It's a bunch of young'uns," he exclaimed. Pointing to the door overhead the man asked, "What's up there?"

"Just the attic," Nora replied.

The man climbed the ladder and shoved his shoulder against the door. He shoved again.

"Papa nailed it shut so our little sister couldn't get up there and fall down," Nora explained.

"Oh," said the man. "Did you young'uns see a black man any time today?"

"No, sir."

"Come on, Pilger, you can see there ain't any black man here," said one of the men in the doorway. "Besides that, I think it was probably Miz Charlotte's hired hand. You know she'll have the sheriff on us if she hears we were a-chasin' him. She claims he's free."

The men backed out of the doorway and the man called Pilger swung the lantern around for one last look.

POOR AS CHURCH MICE

Nora, wrapped in a quilt, slammed the door behind the men and put more wood on the fire. It was a long time before she could sleep. Finally, she scooted down and snuggled against sleeping Amanda when she heard a noise. What if those men had come back, she thought, but she lay very still. Soon steps across the floor made her realize someone had come down from the attic. She was terrified. What could he want?

Lying very still and daring not to breathe, she watched him through slitted eyes. He tiptoed across the room, placed something on the table, took wood from the woodbox and placed it carefully on the fire. A slight flare of the flames showed Nora shiny black skin and short, curly black hair. She watched until he crossed the floor on tiptoe and quietly opened and closed the door. She snuggled down and slept.

CHAPTER 8

The brightly shining sun woke Nora. She rolled over and tried to remember where she was. When she got out of bed and refueled the fire, she saw a small sack on the table. Opening it, she discovered it contained oatmeal. So that was what the black man had placed on the table before he left the sod house.

"Nora," whined Amanda, "I'm hungry."

"Good. Get dressed while I make some oatmeal," replied Nora.

As soon as breakfast was over, Nora and the children repacked the sled and made sure the woodbox in the sod house had been filled. Everything was in order. Settling Amanda on the sled, Nora pulled it toward the pale winter sun.

Walking toward the rising eastern sun, the children plodded until Nora discovered it was overhead. She looked around for a place to prepare lunch.

"Nils," she called, "come on back. We'll rest and eat our lunch in that grove of trees."

"Good, I'm starved," he hollered, pulling the sled toward Nora and Charley. "By the way, Nora, that's called a shelter belt. If a man promised to plant trees on a section of land, he got that land free," explained Nils. "I sure learned lots from Uncle Henley. Amanda, you get up and let Charley under those quilts. I bet you're cold aren't you, Charley?"

Nora looked at Nils in surprise. He had never paid much attention to Charley or Amanda because he was always too busy with Uncle Henley. Amanda whined, but soon was laughing and chasing Nils through the trees.

Nora handed each of them a sandwich. Eating quickly and quietly, Nora repacked the sled where Charley lay.

"Charley, what did you find in the attic of that soddy?" she asked.

Charley sat up quickly, then laid back down. "Nuthin'."

"That's odd," said Nora, "'cause Nils said you were in the attic, but when those men tried to open the door, it seemed to be stuck." Nora looked at him. Her smile was soft and trusting.

"Promise you won't tell anyone, Nora?" he asked.

"Cross my heart and hope to die," promised Nora, crossing the front of her coat.

"There was a black man up there just like those men said, but he said he's a free man. He works for a fine lady called Miz Wagner, both he and his mother. But she's getting too old, so I was thinking maybe we could go there and you could work for her. He said Miz Wagner's farm house isn't too far from here. It's near a country church. Joshua, that's the black man's name, was real friendly, Nora. I'm sure Miz Wagner is, too. Can't we ask someone where it is?" Charley pleaded.

"Charley, it isn't safe to tell people who we are and that we are running away. They would call the sheriff and he'd take us back."

"Nora, we had better get going, hadn't we?" called Nils.

"Yes," replied Nora. "Amanda, you can walk so Nils can pull Charley." She leaned over Charley and asked, "Did you tell Joshua we were out of oatmeal?"

"Yeah," replied Charley settling himself.

Nora and Amanda followed the sled tracks and some horse tracks that appeared to be a road. Some tracks turned off to farmsteads. Did they dare to ask for help in finding Mrs. Wagner's farm like Charley suggested, she wondered?

Nora noticed Charley was no longer riding, and Nils was walking slowly and tiredly. She went to Nils and pulled the sled. Slowly, they followed the tracks headed east. Then Charley began coughing.

"Come on, Charley, and ride again," urged Nora.

"I don't need to. Besides, Nils is too tired to pull me," replied Charley.

"Well, I can pull you."

"No Nora, I'm too heavy for you."

"No you aren't. I'm strong from all the hard work I did at Aunt Augusta's."

"Well," Charley hesitated.

"Hurry up, Amanda has run way ahead, and Nils is too tired to catch her," urged Nora.

Charley sat down, and Nora spread the blanket over him and was tucking it around him when a scream brought her upright. She saw a horseman struggling to lift something onto his horse.

"Amanda!" she screamed and ran toward the group of horsemen. Amanda, in the arms of the rider, was squirming and kicking. The horse danced trying to get away from the child.

"Put her down!" Nora screamed trying to grab Amanda. "You put my sister down."

"Sister? Well now, I thought she was Henley Fairacres' little lost girl. There's a reward out for her you know."

"Uncle Henley?" whispered Nora. "What do you mean Henley Fairacres' lost girl?"

"Aw, come on, Pilger, you know that little girl died nearly ten years ago. The old woman went crazy after that little girl died." He turned to Nora. "Henley's wife once told Pilger she would give him a reward if he found her. He ain't right in the head and remembers things that happened a long time ago and thinks they're true now," explained Pilger's friend. "She told him once she'd pay him fifty dollars if he'd bring her little girl home. Pilger ain't forgot that reward."

"What was her name?" Nora asked in a quiet voice.

The man cocked his head and said, "It was a real pretty name. Something out of a book. Like Air-real."

"Arielle?" Nora asked.

"Yeah, that's it. Airy-ell. Like I said, Pilger thought he could collect that reward on your sister. Don't worry, miss, I won't let him take her. But you best git along home and not stay on the main road no more. Never know when Pilger won't listen to me."

"Thank...thank you, mister," Nora stuttered. She held Amanda close to her.

"I'll give you five dollars if you jest let me have her. Miz Fairacres would take real good care of her," promised Pilger.

Nora picked up Amanda and tried to run with her. Her awkward gait nearly threw them to the snow covered ground.

She struggled on, not waiting for the boys. She heard the man called Pilger laugh and call, "Don't worry, little lady, we'll no doubt meet farther down the road."

Finally, she had to put Amanda down to catch her breath. The boys caught up with her. "We've got to get off the main road." She put Amanda on the sled and hurried across the unbroken stretch of snow.

As it grew dark, Nora looked for a cabin or a building. Anything would do, but all she saw was a stand of trees.

"Nils, I can't see anything but trees to camp in," she said.

"I'll go ahead and find a good spot," offered Nils.

Nora followed pulling the sled. When she got to the trees, Nils had cut branches from the cedars and wove them through the lower branches. Nora and Charley helped him, and before long, they had a snug room of good smelling cedar branches.

"It smells just like Christmas," said Charley, taking a deep breath.

"Not Christmas at Aunt Augusta's," stated Nils.

Nora shook her head, remembering the watery potato soup Aunt Augusta had served them when she wished them Merry Christmas. Her gift to them had been doing their chores. They, in turn, had to do Uncle Henley's chores because he got stranded in town when a blizzard struck.

Nora shook her head to wipe out the unpleasant memory and prepared a bare spot on the ground for a fire. Nils had brought an armload of dry wood. "Nora, where did that small bag of oatmeal come from at the soddy this morning? Aunt Augusta always bought it in ten pound bags."

Nora sat back on her heels. "Do you remember those men who stopped at the soddy last night?"

Nils nodded.

"Well, after they left, I couldn't sleep, and while I lay there, I heard someone. At first I thought it was those men that had been there earlier had come back. But I realized someone had come down from the attic. He left something on the table, and then placed wood on the fire before he left. The fire flared up, and I saw it was a big black man. The oatmeal was on the table when I got up this morning."

"It was Joshua wasn't it?" exclaimed Charley.

"Joshua? Who's Joshua?" asked Nils.

"Joshua is my friend. He was hiding in the attic. I bet he sat on the door so those men couldn't open it. He said he isn't a runaway slave like those men said he was. He works for Miz Wagner who lives near the soddy and near a country church. I wish we could go there. I bet he wouldn't let anyone steal Amanda," said Charley.

"Well, there is no way to find Mrs. Wagner, so we better make our beds here," said Nora.

"Wait, let's use these branches as mattresses. Uncle Henley said that was what they did when they camped out coming from St. Louis," explained Nils.

They slept on fresh smelling greenery and woke to heavily falling snow.

Nora shook the snow off the blanket and discovered the fire was out.

"Nils, Nils, wake up. It's snowing and blowing."

"Good," said Nils sleepily. "We don't have to go to school."

"Nils!" shouted Nora.

"Nora, what's wrong?" whined Amanda.

"It's snowing and blowing, so we can't walk anywhere. And the fire went out. Nils, I only have one match left. What can we do?"

"I guess we'll just have to stay here and hope the weather clears tomorrow. Maybe we should take turns keeping the fire going tonight," suggested Nils.

Nora had them gather more dry wood and clean up the campsite. They then snuggled against each other and told stories. Slowly the day passed. When night came, Nils volunteered to take first watch.

Nora curled up against Amanda and was soon asleep. It seemed a short time later that Nils was tugging at her. She wearily sat up against a tree and watched the fire burning brightly. She sang softly under her breath and told herself stories to keep awake. When she felt her head droop, she took a handful of snow and rubbed her face.

"Nora! Nora! Wake up!"

Nora woke to find Charley shaking her.

"What's wrong, Charley, did the fire go out?" she asked.

"No, but you fell asleep. I'll watch the fire while you sleep."

"Thanks," and she promptly went to sleep.

Nora woke to pale sunshine. Everyone else was sleeping, and the fire was out. Nora felt the ashes, and they were cold. Tears slid down her cheeks. Don't be a fool, she scolded herself silently, all we need is for my tears to freeze my eyes shut.

"Nils, wake up. The fire is out, but the sun is shining, so we can go on."

Nora dug into the food box for bread.

"Nora, I'm thirsty," whined Amanda.

"Don't worry, 'Manda, the creek isn't all frozen over. I'll get you a drink," offered Charley, grabbing the bucket before Nora could stop him.

"Nils, go after him and see that he doesn't fall in," ordered Nora.

But she spoke too late.

"Nora, Nils, help!"

They ran from the shelter to see Charley knee deep in the water. Quickly they found a thick branch and pushed it across the ice. When he grabbed it, they pulled him out. Nora ran ahead and got dry clothes and a blanket for him. Slowly he worked himself into dry clothes. Wrapped in his blanket, he lay on his cedar boughs and shook.

"Nils," Nora said quietly, "you have to find help even if it means going back to Aunt Augusta's."

"No!" shouted Charley. "I'd rather fr-fr-freeze to death than go back there," he stuttered. "I'm sorry I fell asleep and let the fire go out, Nora."

"No, it was my fault. I should have relieved you, Nora," apologized Nils.

"Never mind whose fault it was, just get started, Nils," she scolded. "Which way will you go?"

"North until noon, then east, and angle back south until I get here," said Nils showing Nora drawing in the snow.

Nora dug through the ashes after she had seen Nils on his way, but not a single ember glowed.

She tucked the blankets around Charley and felt his forehead. He was warm. They had to get him into a heated building. In the meantime, she and Amanda would lie on either side of him and keep him warm.

Once again, Nora used the time to tell the younger children about their parents. The morning passed slowly.

Nora tore chunks of the last loaf of bread for lunch.

"I want Aunt Augusta. She has candy for me, not dry old bread," wailed Amanda.

Nora ignored her. She checked Charley's forehead. When she looked into his eyes, she wanted to cry, but said lightly, "Well, Charley, I think your fever is better."

"Yeah, I feel better. Nora, one day I found a magnifying glass on the table and when nobody was looking, I took it."

"Charley!"

Charley hid his head under the covers. Finally he looked at Nora again. "While I was gathering eggs, I set it on the ground near some straw. When I came out of the chicken coop, I saw smoke coming from the straw. Uncle Thomas came into the chicken yard and helped me put the fire out and bury the burned straw. Then he explained the heat of the sun through the glass started the fire. We went out behind the barn and did it again so I could see how it works. But he told me I had to be very careful."

"I wish you had that magnifying glass now," said Nora.

"I do," said Charley. "Uncle Thomas said I could have it, but I'd better not tell Aunt Augusta or she'd make me give it back. I don't think he liked her very much, do you?"

Nora didn't answer. She dug into his wet coat pocket and found the magnifying glass. Searching for the best sunlight shining through the trees, she cleaned the snow off and piled tiny pieces of bark and dried grass. Patiently she held the magnifying glass. Her arm tired, and Charley offered to hold it.

Nora said, "No, I'll rest and try again." Several times Nora held the magnifying glass over the mound of leaves and bark until finally she saw a wisp of smoke. Carefully, she held it steady until she saw a tiny flame, then a larger one. Taking a dry branch, she carried some of the flame to where the fire had been and watched the fire grow. Soon it was blazing, and the tiny shelter warmed.

Nora sat with her arms wrapped around her legs watching Charley and Amanda sleeping. As she peered through the woven branches, she saw Nils walking toward her.

"Nils," she cried, "we got the fire going!" She explained about Charley's magnifying glass. "But what about you? Did you find a building?"

Nils nodded, swallowed a piece of the dry bread, and told Nora about the church he found.

"It's down in a valley. Real pretty. I stood in the trees a long time and watched 'cause there were horse and sleigh tracks leading to it. But finally I decided no one was there, so I went around to the back. There I found a coal chute and slid down into a small room. It was dusty with cobwebs, but no coal or coal dust. I was careful and quiet and looked all through the basement, then went upstairs. It was dusty except for two sets of footprints, one large and one smaller. The smaller pair were smudged like whoever made them dragged their foot. Something else that seemed odd was that it was warm upstairs even though the pews were dusty."

"You're sure no one was there?" Nora asked.

Nils shook his head.

"How far is it?" Nora asked.

"Not far. We should get there before dark."

Nora packed up the sled and woke Charley and Amanda. "Come on, you sleepyheads," she said, "Nils has found a church for us to stay in."

"Is it Joshua's church?" asked Charley in a scratchy voice.

"He's running a fever, too," Nora whispered to Nils.

"Well, is it?" Charley demanded.

"Is it what? Oh, Charley, I don't know. Probably not. It's a long ways from that sod house," said Nils.

"Oh," said Charley, and he lay back down on the cedar boughs.

"Come on, Charley," urged Nora. "Amanda, you'll have to walk. Charley is sick."

Amanda forced a cough. "So am I." She coughed again. "See?" she scrunched herself down on the sled and waited.

"Amanda, did you hear me? I said you would have to walk."

"It's all right, Nora, I can walk," said Charley.

"No, you're not, you can hardly stand. Amanda, get off that sled before I pull you off," demanded Nora.

She hovered over the stubborn girl. "All right, you asked for it!" She grabbed Amanda by the coat collar.

"I can walk, Nora," cried Charley.

"Sit down, Charley. Nils, show us the way," said Nora, ignoring the squalling child on the ground.

"Shut up, Amanda, do you want those men to hear you?"

"No," cried Amanda and ran to catch up with the others. Soon she and Nora were walking hand in hand. Suddenly, Amanda dropped in the snow and began waving her arms and legs.

Nora screamed, "Nils!"

Carefully, Amanda stood up. "Look, Nora. I made a snow angel." Nora began laughing hysterically. Nils came running, his eyes wide with fear.

"I'm sorry, Nils. When Amanda lay down and began waving her arms and legs, I thought she was having some kind of fit. She just made a snow angel."

"Aunt Augusta taught me how to make them," explained Amanda.

Soon Amanda was tired of making snow angels, and Nora was glad when Nils shouted to her. Hurrying to join him, Nora noticed he had pulled the sled into a stand of trees. Pulling Amanda along behind her, Nora stood beside Nils.

"What's wrong, Nils? Is someone there?"

"No," said Nils. "But I was just thinking, if anyone came this way they would see our footprints."

"And Amanda's snow angels."

"No," cried Amanda. "Those are my snow angels."

Nora ignored her and struggled to erase the deep indentations until she heard Nils yell she had gone far enough. Carefully, she brushed a branch across the snow until she bumped into the sled. She followed the others down the hill and across the valley, wiping out any evidence of their trespassing.

The opening in the coal chute was too small for the sled to be slid through, so Nora unpacked it and had Nils hide it in a woodpile a few feet from the church.

She slid down the chute and then caught Amanda and Charley when Nils helped them. Stacking their boxes and bundles in a small room just off the coal room, they began exploring the basement.

There was a large room with broken pews. One was minus an end and another had a large crack across the back. Two were wobbly. There was a table and two spindle chairs and two high-backed chairs with worn velvet seats.

"Nils, what if they come downstairs and see our footprints?" asked Nora.

"I don't think they ever come downstairs because there were no footprints on the floor when I came in," explained Nils.

Nora dug into the lunch box and handed everyone a piece of dried beef to chew on. She moved the pews together to make beds.

"I want to go upstairs, Nora. Nils said it was warm up there," whined Amanda.

"We can't, Amanda. Someone might come, and they'd take us back to Aunt Augusta's. Come on, I have a bed ready for us," replied Nora, pointing to the pews she had pushed together and spread with their blankets.

Nora woke to footsteps overhead. It took her a minute to remember where she was. She saw Nils sit up. Silently, they listened. Soon they heard a door open and close. Nora motioned for Nils to go to the top of the stairs. She sat with her finger to her lips when she saw Charley sit up. Soon the basement door opened, and Nils came down the stairs.

"Well?" she whispered.

"You don't have to whisper. There isn't anyone up there, and a fire is going. It is as clean as a whistle. No cobwebs or dust on the floor or pews," Nils reported.

"What do you make of it?" Nora asked, still whispering afraid someone might hear them talking.

"Don't know, but now we can go upstairs and not worry," he replied.

"And get warm," said Charley.

They traipsed upstairs and stared at the stained-glass windows and shiny pews. They huddled beside the stove. Suddenly Nora said, "Hush, I thought I heard something."

"Oh, you're just spooked," sneered Nils.

Nora hit his arm. Suddenly, they heard someone singing loudly, then yell, "Whoa."

They hastily gathered up their things and raced for the stairs. Just as they crawled into the small room off the coal room, they heard the front door open above them.

Huddled together, they waited. Soon they heard a strong high-pitched voice, "So, this is what took you so long this morning to light the stove. Are we expecting company in our little unused church?"

"No," replied a deep voice. "I jest got tired of seeing cobwebs in your hair and dust all over your go-to-meetin' coat."

"Joshua!" cried Charley.

Nora clapped her hand over his mouth.

They all held their breath.

"What was that?" asked the voice above them.

"I di'n't hear nuthin'," replied the deep voice.

"Did you trap those mice like I told you?"

"Now, Miz Charlotte, yo' know if you tells ol' Josh to do somethin', I does it."

"Well, then, Mr. Josh, you tell me what I just heard if it wasn't a mouse."

"Maybe it was a church mouse. You know there ain't nuthin' poorer than a church mouse."

"Oh, you old fool, stop twaddling and start walking. I still think this walking round and round this church is a waste of time. How is walking supposed to help a broken leg?" asked the high-pitched voice.

"Your leg ain't broke no more, Miz Charlotte. It needs ex-er-cise or somethin'. And you sure can't walk around your house for exercise. Too much furniture. What you ever gonna do with all that furniture?"

"None of your business, you nosy old fool. Now be quiet and let me concentrate on my ex-er-ci-sing."

Nora listened quietly to the footsteps as they grew fainter and then louder. Nearly an hour had passed when Nora realized the people were preparing to leave the church.

"Joshua, wait for me. You know I can't walk through that snow without holding onto you," Nora heard Miz Charlotte say.

The deep voice replied, "You jest sit and rest yourself on that shiny clean pew. I'se goin' for some mo' wood for the heatin' stove. You neber know, them church mice jest might need it."

"Humph," snorted Miz Charlotte.

Soon the upstairs was empty, and Nora hurried the others to the warmth of the stove.

The next two days passed quickly. Nora and the others spent their time searching through the church and found a sack of food addressed to: "The Church Mice."

"Nils, I think today could be Sunday," said Nora, the third day they had been there. "Do you think we should leave the church in case people come to worship? They might wander down here, even bring food to have a pot luck dinner."

"We'll see if anybody comes to start the fire. If they do, we'll hide in the trees," suggested Nils.

They waited patiently all morning, all packed up to move if necessary. Slowly, they relaxed, built a fire, and enjoyed the warmth and freedom.

"Nils, Charley is much better. I think we can start again for Omaha. I wonder what Aunt Augusta and Uncle Henley are doing," Nora said.

"Who cares?" blurted out Charley. "Nora, what was in that bundle Uncle Thomas put in the bottom of our clothes bag?"

"What bundle?" Nora asked.

"It looked like a packet of letters. I couldn't see too well as I had to pretend I was asleep 'cause Uncle Thomas thought I was. It was the day I had the croup, and Uncle Henley sent me back to bed. Boy, wasn't Aunt Augusta mad? She had to carry her own wood."

Nora quickly dug in the clean clothes bag. At the very bottom, she found a packet of letters tied with a piece of string. They were addressed to Nora. She shuffled through them and found the first postmark and began sorting them. "They're from Mama! She started writing about three months after we left. Aunt Augusta opened them. I wonder if she answered them," said Nora.

Nils picked one up from the pile that was unopened. "No," he said, "this one is dated October."

Slowly they sorted them all, and Nora read them aloud. The letters told that their mother slowly recovered her health. Officer O'Herrity had visited her often and encouraged her to try to get well so she could join the children. Then, he arranged for her to work at the orphanage as her health improved. Mother Superior promised her she could accompany the next trainload of children going to Nebraska. She was saving all the money she earned so she and the children could live together. She probably could find work in one of the towns near Aunt Augusta and Uncle Henley because they had been so good to the children and had given them such wonderful care.

The unopened letters spoke more of her worry about not receiving answers to her letters. She still spoke of the plan of making a home for her children. She wished she had an address of someone living near Uncle Henley so they could let her know the children were well and happy.

Tears ran down Nora's face. "Poor Mama," she said. "Nils, we have to get to Omaha and send a telegram to Mama so she'll know we are well."

"Yeah," he mumbled hoarsely, his back turned to her.

They spent the evening sorting through the clothing. Nils found a bucket and filled it with snow so Nora could rinse out their clothing and hang it around the stove to dry. She repacked the food that had been brought daily to the church with a note always attached that read: "for the poor Church Mice." If they were careful, they would be able to eat for three days. And if they could find a ride, they would take it because they had to let Mama know they were well and waiting for her in Omaha. Nora knew she and the boys could find work in Omaha while they waited for Mama to arrive. With a much happier heart, Nora packed for their trip.

She fell asleep saying her prayers and had to smile, for a church was the perfect place to pray.

CHAPTER 9

Nora woke early. She was so happy she began to sing. At first, her happy voice startled her. Then she remembered they were soon going to see Mama. A twittering bird whistled with her song. Charley! Then she looked at Nils. He wore his ear-to-ear smile. Their crowning glories! Suddenly she remembered the terrible haircut. Her crowning glory was gone, but it would soon grown back. Even now, it was no longer jagged and spiky, but had grown enough for Nils to trim and shape it evenly. Nora looked at Amanda. What was her crowning glory?

"Nora, I'm hungry."

"Whining, that's your crowning glory, Amanda. That's the gift Aunt Augusta gave you. But don't you worry, Mama will find a much nicer one. Come on, our secret friend left us a bag of oatmeal," said Nora.

"It's Joshua, Nora. You know it is 'cause he called us church mice when he was here with Miz Charlotte," replied Charley.

"I suppose it is Joshua. I'd like to thank him before we leave," commented Nora.

"Maybe we could leave him a note," suggested Charlie.

"Nils, are you ready for breakfast?" called Nora to her brother standing in the doorway.

"Shhh. Come here and listen. I think I hear someone calling."

Nora stood beside Nils and strained to listen. "That's just the wind in the trees," she said and started back into the room.

"Nora, wait, now listen." Once again Nora strained to hear a voice.

After a moment she said, "You know, Nils, I think someone is calling. We'd better go see."

Cautioning Charley and Amanda to stay in the church, Nora and Nils began their search. Abruptly they came upon sleigh tracks across the white field of snow. They followed them until they saw a sleigh overturned. A leg, twisted at an odd angle, was sticking out from beneath it.

"Nils, look, someone is underneath the sleigh."

"Yeah, but where's the horse?" asked Nils, as he studied the tracks.

"I cut him loose. I hoped he'd stop at the church."

"Joshua!" cried Nils.

Grasping the side of the sleigh, Nora and Nils lifted. Slowly a large man slid out, his face twisted in pain. Pushing harder, they were able to set the sleigh upright.

"You are Joshua, aren't you?" asked Nora.

"Yessum, and I thank you for rescuing me. You must be Nora and Nils, Charley's big sister and brother," he said with a grunt.

"Nils, we have to get him back to the church, but how? We can't carry him."

"No, miss, that you can't. But if you cut a thick branch, I can hop. Nils, if you look in the sleigh, you'll find an axe."

"Maybe we could bring the sled here and pull you to the church," suggested Nora.

"You two itty-bitty people pull big, handsome Joshua on a little bitty sled? No thank'ee. I'll hop," replied Josh in his booming voice.

Nora helped Nils clean the branches off the stout limb and situate it under Joshua's arm.

"Nils, you walk beside him so he can lean on you. I'll run ahead and stir up the fire. We were planning on leaving this morning, so we let the fire burn down," she explained to Joshua.

Nora hurried through the snow. Not far from the church, she saw Charley pulling the sled. "Charley, didn't I tell you to stay with Amanda?" she cried angrily.

"Yes, but someone was yelling for help, and I thought you and Nils might need the sled," explained Charley.

"What about Amanda?" she asked.

"She's back there whining as usual," replied Charley.

"Well, go back there with her. Add two sticks of wood to the stove. Just two pieces, mind you."

"But did you find somebody?" cried Charley.

"Yes, Joshua had a sleigh accident. I'll pull the sled back. Maybe he'll try riding on it for a little ways to rest."

"Nora, I want to help. He was my friend first. Remember the sodhouse?"

"Charley, he's a big man. It will take Nils and me to pull him. You can help best by warming the church. He is chilled clear through. Now, go get Amanda back inside. Here she comes, and she doesn't even have her coat on!" Nora took the sled rope and gave Charley a shove toward the church. "Amanda, you get yourself back into the church right now!" she hollered.

Nora pulled the sled toward Nils and Joshua. She met them as they were resting. Joshua's chocolate brown face was sweaty and patchy gray from the pain of his injured leg.

"Charley was bringing the sled to you, Joshua. He'd be very disappointed if you didn't at least try riding on it."

Joshua gave her a painful smile and lowered himself onto it. The sled, which had seemed so large when Amanda or Charley rode on it, seemed to shrink in size as Joshua settled himself.

Nora and Nils began pulling. Soon they stopped to rest. Nora looked back at Joshua, ready to assure him he didn't need to walk again. He seemed to be sleeping.

They finally reached the church and, with great effort, they got Joshua up the steps and into the warm building. Charley had placed a pillow and quilt on a pew.

"We're almost there, Joshua," encouraged Nora, as they struggled to get the big man down without hurting his leg. "Nils, you have to go for help. Joshua, can you tell Nils how to get to Mrs. Charlotte's?" Nora asked.

She knew the man needed rest, but he also needed help. Nils sat beside the injured man who drew a map.

"Nils, how much would it cost to send Mama a telegram?" Nora asked.

"What does it matter? We don't have any money."

"Well, I thought Mrs. Charlotte would pay me to do some housework, or maybe she would let you do some of Joshua's work until he was better," suggested Nora.

The morning passed slowly with the children playing quietly, so Joshua would sleep.

"Nora, I'm hungry," whined Amanda.

Nora tried to hush her. She had packed all the food for their trip, except for a little she had planned to use for their noon meal, and it wasn't quite noon.

Nora heard Joshua moan. "Can I help you?" she asked.

"No. I jest remembered I had a basket of food in the sleigh for my pet church mice. Can Charley go get it?" the injured man asked.

"Charley, come here, please," called Nora.

After receiving instructions of what to look for, Nora took Charley to the doorway. "See our tracks? Stay with them and you will find the sleigh. It was tipped over so the basket probably fell out. Just keep the sleigh in sight while you look and then follow the tracks back."

"I'm not a baby like Amanda, Nora, I know about following tracks and not getting lost," Charley replied indignantly.

Noon came, and Nora fixed a hot meal from the food in the basket Charley had found.

Nora was reading a book to Amanda when she heard Charley ask Joshua if he liked to sing. Soon they were singing hymns together; Charley in a clear, high soprano, and Joshua in a deep bass. Nora was so enthralled, she didn't hear the door open, but the stamping of feet caught her attention, and she turned to see a man with a little black bag. Behind him was Nils and two women.

"Nils, you're back!" she cried happily.

"Nora, this is Mrs. Charlotte Wagner and her housekeeper, Mrs. Anna Slocum. Mrs. Slocum is Joshua's mother. These are my sisters, Nora and Amanda, Mrs. Wagner. My brother, Charley is over there with Joshua."

Nora curtsied to the women. "Won't you come in, ladies?" she asked, offering to take their coats.

"Thank you, Nora," said Mrs. Wagner shrugging out of her coat. "We're anxious to hear what the doctor has to say about Joshua." Holding on to each other, they hurried to where Joshua lay.

"Charley, come out of the doctor's way," Nora called. She watched as the three adults conversed, then she asked, "Can we help?"

"Thank you, no," replied Mrs. Wagner. "The doctor thinks he can help Joshua out to his sleigh."

"Amanda, Charley, come, let's get our coats on. Nils, you go get the sled."

When they were all ready, Nora herded the children to Joshua. "Excuse us, please. We are going now, but first we want to thank Joshua for all the help he gave us while we waited here for Charley to get well enough to travel."

"Going?" exclaimed Mrs. Wagner. "What do you mean going? And where are you going?"

"To Omaha to meet our mother," replied Nora.

Mrs. Wagner's gruff manner scared Nora, so she decided she would not ask for work, but go to Omaha and seek help from Beth's new family.

"No such thing!" snapped Mrs. Wagner. "You are going home with me. Dr. Ridley will send a message to your mother and to your aunt and uncle, that you are well."

Nora's face fell and tears streamed down her cheeks.

Charley stomped to Mrs. Wagner and looked ferociously at her and cried, "We are not going back to Aunt Augusta's! She's mean. Do you know what she did to Nora's hair?"

"Hush, Charley, it doesn't matter," said Nora.

"Go back? No one said anything about going back to your aunt and uncle. I know Augusta and a meaner woman never lived. And yes, Nils told me all about your troubles," replied Mrs. Wagner.

"Nils!" scolded Nora.

"Oh, don't scold the boy. I nagged it out of him. I'm good at that," said Mrs. Wagner.

"That's right so, Miss Nora," muttered Joshua.

"Hush, you fool. Anyone who will tip over a sleigh just because the horse probably shied at a rabbit is a no-account," said Mrs. Wagner.

Nora saw a grin on Joshua's face as he looked fondly at his employer. She listened in amazement as Mrs. Wagner said, "Nils, take the horse you rode and hitch it to the sleigh Joshua tipped over, then bring it to the church. When you get the children and your boxes and bags loaded, you come to my house." She turned to Nora, "Don't get any ideas about driving off to Omaha. You can come and stay with me. We'll telegraph your mother not to wait for the Orphan Train, but get on the next train to Omaha. That is, if she'll accept my offer to be my housekeeper. Mrs. Slocum's rheumatism is getting so bad, she isn't able to take care of us properly anymore. You can live with me in the big house until Joshua is well enough to fix up the tenant house. Nora, you can take your mother's place till she arrives. Then, I expect all of you to go to school. Oh yes, Nils, you'll have to do Joshua's work until he is able."

"Me too," cried Charley.

"Thank you," whispered Nora. "Just think, Nils, we can be a family again. You and Charley and Amanda and me with Mama! If Mama agrees to work as Mrs. Wagner's housekeeper, she won't have to look for work outside the home, and we can go back to school. A family, a family," she sang, as she danced her brothers and sister around the room.

"No more being poor church mice," sang Charley.

"And maybe we can find a nicer crowning glory for Amanda than whining," said Nils.

"Can I change my name to Arielle?" asked Amanda.

"NO!" shouted the children.

"Can I be a substitute grandmother?" asked Mrs. Wagner.

"YES!" shouted the children. This time Amanda joined in.

About the Author

When Roselyn Ogden Miller read of the "empty nest syndrome," she feared it. Probably because she was raised with six siblings and is the mother of five children. So even before her oldest child left home, she began her fight against it with a babysitting service in her home. Then came foster children, foreign exchange students from Sweden, Denmark, Mexico, and France and, last but not least, licensed child daycare, where she cared for more than a hundred children over a twenty year span.

Roselyn and her husband, Allen are retired and spend their time with their five children, in-law-children and thirteen grandchildren. Her interests are varied: golfing, embroidering, reading (history is a favorite subject) and volunteering her services to various committees. She is also active in her church.